A Heap o' Livin'

A Heap o' Livin'

By
Edgar A. Guest

 LIGHTHOUSE PRESS
FARMINGDALE NY

Republished 1977

International Standard Book Number: 0-89968-041-0
Library of Congress Catalog Card Number 80-84108

For ordering information, contact:

LIGHTHOUSE PRESS
Box 245, Farmingdale, NY 11735

To
Marjorie and Buddy
this little book of verse
is affectionately
dedicated
by their Daddy

INDEX

Index

Index

Index

WHEN YOU KNOW A FELLOW

When you get to know a fellow, know his joys
    and know his cares,
When you've come to understand him and the
    burdens that he bears,
When you've learned the fight he's making and
    the troubles in his way,
Then you find that he is different than you
    thought him yesterday.
You find his faults are trivial and there's not so
    much to blame
In the brother that you jeered at when you only
    knew his name.

You are quick to see the blemish in the distant
    neighbor's style,
You can point to all his errors and may sneer
    at him the while,
And your prejudices fatten and your hates
    more violent grow
As you talk about the failures of the man you
    do not know,
But when drawn a little closer, and your hands
    and shoulders touch,
You find the traits you hated really don't
    amount to much.

When you get to know a fellow, know his every
    mood and whim,
You begin to find the texture of the splendid
    side of him;
You begin to understand him, and you cease to
    scoff and sneer,
For with understanding always prejudices dis-
    appear.
You begin to find his virtues and his faults you
    cease to tell,
For you seldom hate a fellow when you know
    him very well.

When next you start in sneering and your
    phrases turn to blame,
Know more of him you censure than his business
    and his name;
For it's likely that acquaintance would your
    prejudice dispel
And you'd really come to like him if you
    knew him very well.
When you get to know a fellow and you under-
    stand his ways,
Then his faults won't really matter, for you'll
    find a lot to praise.

THE ROUGH LITTLE RASCAL

A smudge on his nose and a smear on his cheek
And knees that might not have been washed in
      a week;
A bump on his forehead, a scar on his lip,
A relic of many a tumble and trip:
A rough little, tough little rascal, but sweet,
Is he that each evening I'm eager to meet.

A brow that is beady with jewels of sweat;
A face that's as black as a visage can get;
A suit that at noon was a garment of white,
Now one that his mother declares is a fright:
A fun-loving, sun-loving rascal, and fine,
Is he that comes placing his black fist in mine.

A crop of brown hair that is tousled and tossed;
A waist from which two of the buttons are lost;
A smile that shines out through the dirt and the
      grime,
And eyes that are flashing delight all the time:
All these are the joys that I'm eager to meet
And look for the moment I get to my street

IT ISN'T COSTLY

Does the grouch get richer quicker than the
    friendly sort of man?
Can the grumbler labor better than the cheerful
    fellow can?
Is the mean and churlish neighbor any cleverer
    than the one
Who shouts a glad " good morning," and then
    smiling passes on?

Just stop and think about it. Have you ever
    known or seen
A mean man who succeeded, just because he
    was so mean?
When you find a grouch with honors and with
    money in his pouch,
You can bet he didn't win them just because
    he was a grouch.

Oh, you'll not be any poorer if you smile along
    your way,
And your lot will not be harder for the kindly
    things you say.
Don't imagine you are wasting time for others
    that you spend:
You can rise to wealth and glory and still pause
    to be a friend.

MY CREED

To live as gently as I can;
To be, no matter where, a man;
To take what comes of good or ill
And cling to faith and honor still;
To do my best, and let that stand
The record of my brain and hand;
And then, should failure come to me,
Still work and hope for victory.

To have no secret place wherein
I stoop unseen to shame or sin;
To be the same when I'm alone
As when my every deed is known;
To live undaunted, unafraid
Of any step that I have made;
To be without pretense or sham
Exactly what men think I am.

To leave some simple mark behind
To keep my having lived in mind;
If enmity to aught I show,
To be an honest, generous foe,
To play my little part, nor whine
That greater honors are not mine.
This, I believe, is all I need,
For my philosophy and creed.

A WISH

I'd like to be a boy again, a care-free prince of
    joy again,
  I'd like to tread the hills and dales the way I
    used to do;
I'd like the tattered shirt again, the knickers
    thick with dirt again,
  The ugly, dusty feet again that long ago I
    knew.
I'd like to play first base again, and Sliver's
    curves to face again,
  I'd like to climb, the way I did, a friendly
    apple tree;
For, knowing what I do to-day, could I but
    wander back and play,
  I'd get full measure of the joy that boy-
    hood gave to me.

I'd like to be a lad again, a youngster, wild and
    glad again,
  I'd like to sleep and eat again the way I used
    to do;
I'd like to race and run again, and drain from
    life its fun again,
  And start another round of joy the moment
    one was through.
But care and strife have come to me, and often
    days are glum to me,

And sleep is not the thing it was and food
is not the same;
And I have sighed, and known that I must
journey on again to sigh,
And I have stood at envy's point and heard
the voice of shame.

I've learned that joys are fleeting things; that
parting pain each meeting brings;
That gain and loss are partners here, and so
are smiles and tears;
That only boys from day to day can drain and
fill the cup of play;
That age must mourn for what is lost
throughout the coming years.
But boys cannot appreciate their priceless joy
until too late
And those who own the charms I had will
soon be changed to men;
And then, they too will sit, as I, and backward
turn to look and sigh
And share my longing, vain, to be a care-
free boy again.

WHAT A BABY COSTS

"How much do babies cost?" said he
The other night upon my knee;
And then I said: "They cost a lot;
A lot of watching by a cot,
A lot of sleepless hours and care,
A lot of heart-ache and despair,
A lot of fear and trying dread,
And sometimes many tears are shed
In payment for our babies small,
But every one is worth it all.

"For babies people have to pay
A heavy price from day to day —
There is no way to get one cheap.
Why, sometimes when they're fast asleep
You have to get up in the night
And go and see that they're all right.
But what they cost in constant care
And worry, does not half compare
With what they bring of joy and bliss —
You'd pay much more for just a kiss.

"Who buys a baby has to pay
A portion of the bill each day;
He has to give his time and thought
Unto the little one he's bought.
He has to stand a lot of pain
Inside his heart and not complain;

And pay with lonely days and sad
For all the happy hours he's had.
All this a baby costs, and yet
His smile is worth it all, you bet."

MOTHER

Never a sigh for the cares that she bore for me,
  Never a thought of the joys that flew by;
Her one regret that she couldn't do more for me,
  Thoughtless and selfish, her Master was I.

Oh, the long nights that she came at my call to
    me!
  Oh, the soft touch of her hands on my brow!
Oh, the long years that she gave up her all to
    me!
  Oh, how I yearn for her gentleness now!

Slave to her baby! Yes, that was the way of
    her,
  Counting her greatest of services small;
Words cannot tell what this old heart would
    say of her,
  Mother — the sweetest and fairest of all.

SELFISH

I am selfish in my wishin' every sort o' joy for
 you;
I am selfish when I tell you that I'm wishin'
 skies o' blue
Bending o'er you every minute, and a pocketful
 of gold,
An' as much of love an' gladness as a human
 heart can hold.
Coz I know beyond all question that if such a
 thing could be
As you cornerin' life's riches you would share
 'em all with me.

I am selfish in my wishin' every sorrow from
 your way,
With no trouble thoughts to fret you at the
 closin' o' the day;
An' it's selfishness that bids me wish you com-
 forts by the score,
An' all the joys you long for, an' on top o'
 them, some more;
Coz I know, old tried an' faithful, that if such
 a thing could be
As you cornerin' life's riches you would share
 'em all with me.

RICH

Who has a troop of romping youth
  About his parlor floor,
Who nightly hears a round of cheers,
  When he is at the door,
Who is attacked on every side
  By eager little hands
That reach to tug his grizzled mug,
  The wealth of earth commands.

Who knows the joys of girls and boys,
  His lads and lassies, too,
Who's pounced upon and bounced upon
  When his day's work is through,
Whose trousers know the gentle tug
  Of some glad little tot,
The baby of his crew of love,
  Is wealthier than a lot.

Oh, be he poor and sore distressed
  And weary with the fight,
If with a whoop his healthy troop
  Run, welcoming at night,
And kisses greet him at the end
  Of all his toiling grim,
With what is best in life he's blest
  And rich men envy him.

MA AND THE AUTO

Before we take an auto ride Pa says to Ma:
    " My dear,
Now just remember I don't need suggestions
    from the rear.
If you will just sit still back there and hold
    in check your fright,
I'll take you where you want to go and get
    you back all right.
Remember that my hearing's good and also I'm
    not blind,
And I can drive this car without suggestions
    from behind."

Ma promises that she'll keep still, then off we
    gayly start,
But soon she notices ahead a peddler and his
    cart.
" You'd better toot your horn," says she, " to let
    him know we're near;
He might turn out! " and Pa replies: " Just
    shriek at him, my dear."
And then he adds: " Some day, some guy will
    make a lot of dough
By putting horns on tonneau seats for women-
    folks to blow! "

A little farther on Ma cries: "He signaled for
a turn!"
And Pa says: "Did he?" in a tone that's hot
enough to burn.
"Oh, there's a boy on roller skates!" cries Ma.
"Now do go slow.
I'm sure he doesn't see our car." And Pa says:
"I dunno,
I think I don't need glasses yet, but really it
may be
That I am blind and cannot see what's right
in front of me."

If Pa should speed the car a bit some rigs to
hurry past
Ma whispers: "Do be careful now. You're
driving much too fast."
And all the time she's pointing out the dangers
of the street
And keeps him posted on the roads where
trolley cars he'll meet.
Last night when we got safely home, Pa sighed
and said: "My dear,
I'm sure we've all enjoyed the drive you gave
us from the rear!"

ON GOING HOME FOR CHRISTMAS

He little knew the sorrow that was in his vacant
    chair;
He never guessed they'd miss him, or he'd
    surely have been there;
He couldn't see his mother or the lump that
    filled her throat,
Or the tears that started falling as she read
    his hasty note;
And he couldn't see his father, sitting sor-
    rowful and dumb,
Or he never would have written that he thought
    he couldn't come.

He little knew the gladness that his presence
    would have made,
And the joy it would have given, or he never
    would have stayed.
He didn't know how hungry had the little
    mother grown
Once again to see her baby and to claim him
    for her own.
He didn't guess the meaning of his visit
    Christmas Day
Or he never would have written that he
    couldn't get away.

He couldn't see the fading of the cheeks that
 once were pink,
And the silver in the tresses; and he didn't
 stop to think
How the years are passing swiftly, and next
 Christmas it might be
There would be no home to visit and no mother
 dear to see.
He didn't think about it — I'll not say he didn't
 care.
He was heedless and forgetful or he'd surely
 have been there.

Are you going home for Christmas? Have you
 written you'll be there?
Going home to kiss the mother and to show
 her that you care?
Going home to greet the father in a way to
 make him glad?
If you're not I hope there'll never come a time
 you'll wish you had.
Just sit down and write a letter — it will make
 their heart strings hum
With a tune of perfect gladness — if you'll tell
 them that you'll come.

AT SUGAR CAMP

At Sugar Camp the cook is kind
  And laughs the laugh we knew as boys;
And there we slip away and find
  Awaiting us the old-time joys.
The catbird calls the selfsame way
  She used to in the long ago,
And there's a chorus all the day
  Of songsters it is good to know.

The killdeer in the distance cries;
  The thrasher, in her garb of brown,
From tree to tree in gladness flies.
  Forgotten is the world's renown,
Forgotten are the years we've known;
  At Sugar Camp there are no men;
We've ceased to strive for things to own;
  We're in the woods as boys again.

Our pride is in the strength of trees,
  Our pomp the pomp of living things;
Our ears are tuned to melodies
  That every feathered songster sings.
At Sugar Camp our noonday meal
  Is eaten in the open air,
Where through the leaves the sunbeams steal
  And simple is our bill of fare.

At Sugar Camp in peace we dwell
   And none is boastful of himself;
None plots to gain with shot and shell
   His neighbor's bit of land or pelf.
The roar of cannon isn't heard,
   There stilled is money's tempting voice;
Someone detects a new-come bird
   And at her presence all rejoice.

At Sugar Camp the cook is kind;
   His steak is broiling o'er the coals
And in its sputtering we find
   Sweet harmony for tired souls.
There, sheltered by the friendly trees,
   As boys we sit to eat our meal,
And, brothers to the birds and bees,
   We hold communion with the real.

HOME

It takes a heap o' livin' in a house t' make it
    home,
A heap o' sun an' shadder, an' ye sometimes
    have t' roam
Afore ye really 'preciate the things ye lef'
    behind,
An' hunger fer 'em somehow, with 'em allus
    on yer mind.
It don't make any differunce how rich ye get
    t' be,
How much yer chairs an' tables cost, how great
    yer luxury;
It ain't home t' ye, though it be the palace of a
    king,
Until somehow yer soul is sort o' wrapped round
    everything.

Home ain't a place that gold can buy or get up
    in a minute;
Afore it's home there's got t' be a heap o' livin'
    in it;
Within the walls there's got t' be some babies
    born, and then
Right there ye've got t' bring 'em up t' women
    good, an' men;
And gradjerly, as time goes on, ye find ye
    wouldn't part

With anything they ever used — they've grown
    into yer heart:
The old high chairs, the playthings, too, the
    little shoes they wore
Ye hoard; an' if ye could ye'd keep the thumb-
    marks on the door.

Ye've got t' weep t' make it home, ye've got t'
    sit an' sigh
An' watch beside a loved one's bed, an' know
    that Death is nigh;
An' in the stillness o' the night t' see Death's
    angel come,
An' close the eyes o' her that smiled, an' leave
    her sweet voice dumb.
Fer these are scenes that grip the heart, an'
    when yer tears are dried,
Ye find the home is dearer than it was, an'
    sanctified;
An' tuggin' at ye always are the pleasant
    memories
O' her that was an' is no more — ye can't escape
    from these.

Ye've got t' sing an' dance fer years, ye've got
    t' romp an' play,
An' learn t' love the things ye have by usin' 'em
    each day;
Even the roses 'round the porch must blossom
    year by year

Afore they 'come a part o' ye, suggestin'
    someone dear
Who used t' love 'em long ago, an' trained 'em
    jes' t' run
The way they do, so's they would get the early
    mornin' sun;
Ye've got t' love each brick an' stone from
    cellar up t' dome:
It takes a heap o' livin' in a house t' make it
    home.

THE PATH THAT LEADS TO HOME

The little path that leads to home,
    That is the road for me,
I know no finer path to roam,
    With finer sights to see.
With thoroughfares the world is lined
    That lead to wonders new,
But he who treads them leaves behind
    The tender things and true.

Oh, north and south and east and west
    The crowded roadways go,
And sweating brow and weary breast
    Are all they seem to know.
And mad for pleasure some are bent,
    And some are seeking fame,

And some are sick with discontent,
    And some are bruised and lame.

Across the world the gleaming steel
    Holds out its lure for men,
But no one finds his comfort real
    Till he comes home again.
And charted lanes now line the sea
    For weary hearts to roam,
But, Oh, the finest path to me
    Is that which leads to home.

'Tis there I come to laughing eyes
    And find a welcome true;
'Tis there all care behind me lies
    And joy is ever new.
And, Oh, when every day is done
    Upon that little street,
A pair of rosy youngsters run
    To me with flying feet.

The world with myriad paths is lined
    But one alone for me,
One little road where I may find
    The charms I want to see.
Though thoroughfares majestic call
    The multitude to roam,
I would not leave, to know them all,
    The path that leads to home.

A FRIEND'S GREETING

I'd like to be the sort of friend that you have
    been to me;
I'd like to be the help that you've been always
    glad to be;
I'd like to mean as much to you each minute
    of the day
As you have meant, old friend of mine, to me
    along the way.

I'd like to do the big things and the splendid
    things for you,
To brush the gray from out your skies and
    leave them only blue;
I'd like to say the kindly things that I so oft
    have heard,
And feel that I could rouse your soul the way
    that mine you've stirred.

I'd like to give you back the joy that you have
    given me,
Yet that were wishing you a need I hope will
    never be;
I'd like to make you feel as rich as I, who
    travel on
Undaunted in the darkest hours with you to
    lean upon.

I'm wishing at this Christmas time that I could
      but repay
A portion of the gladness that you've strewn
      along my way;
And could I have one wish this year, this only
      would it be:
I'd like to be the sort of friend that you have
      been to me.

A SONG

None knows the day that friends must part.
  None knows how near is sorrow;
If there be laughter in your heart,
  Don't hold it for to-morrow.
Smile all the smiles you can to-day;
Grief waits for all along the way.

To-day is ours for joy and mirth;
  We may be sad to-morrow;
Then let us sing for all we're worth,
  Nor give a thought to sorrow.
None knows what lies along the way;
Let's smile what smiles we can to-day.

OLD FRIENDS

I do not say new friends are not considerate and
    true,
Or that their smiles ain't genuine, but still I'm
    tellin' you
That when a feller's heart is crushed and achin'
    with the pain,
And teardrops come a-splashin' down his cheeks
    like summer rain,
Becoz his grief an' loneliness are more than
    he can bear,
Somehow it's only old friends, then, that really
    seem to care.
The friends who've stuck through thick an'
    thin, who've known you, good an' bad,
Your faults an' virtues, an' have seen the strug-
    gles you have had,
When they come to you gentle-like an' take
    your hand an' say:
"Cheer up! we're with you still," it counts, for
    that's the old friends' way.

The new friends may be fond of you for what
    you are to-day;
They've only known you rich, perhaps, an' only
    seen you gay;
You can't tell what's attracted them; your
    station may appeal;

Perhaps they smile on you because you're doin'
    something real;
But old friends who have seen you fail, an' also
    seen you win,
Who've loved you either up or down, stuck
    to you, thick or thin,
Who knew you as a budding youth, an' watched
    you start to climb,
Through weal an' woe, still friends of yours
    an' constant all the time,
When trouble comes an' things go wrong, I
    don't care what you say,
They are the friends you'll turn to, for you
    want the old friends' way.

The new friends may be richer, an' more stylish,
    too, but when
Your heart is achin' an' you think your sun
    won't shine again,
It's not the riches of new friends you want, it's
    not their style,
It's not the airs of grandeur then, it's just the
    old friend's smile,
The old hand that has helped before, stretched
    out once more to you,
The old words ringin' in your ears, so sweet an',
    Oh, so true!
The tenderness of folks who know just what
    your sorrow means,

These are the things on which, somehow, your
    spirit always leans.
When grief is poundin' at your breast — the
    new friends disappear
An' to the old ones tried an' true, you turn for
    aid an' cheer.

FOLKS

We was speakin' of folks, jes' common folks,
    An' we come to this conclusion,
That wherever they be, on land or sea,
    They warm to a home allusion;
That under the skin an' under the hide
    There's a spark that starts a-glowin'
Whenever they look at a scene or book
    That something of home is showin'.

They may differ in creeds an' politics,
    They may argue an' even quarrel,
But their throats grip tight, if they catch a
    sight
Of their favorite elm or laurel.
An' the winding lane that they used to tread
    With never a care to fret 'em,
Or the pasture gate where they used to wait,
    Right under the skin will get 'em.

Now folks is folks on their different ways,
  With their different griefs an' pleasures,
But the home they knew, when their years were
      few,
  Is the dearest of all their treasures.
An' the richest man to the poorest waif
  Right under the skin is brother
When they stand an' sigh, with a tear-dimmed
      eye,
  At a thought of the dear old mother.

It makes no difference where it may be,
  Nor the fortunes that years may alter,
Be they simple or wise, the old home ties
  Make all of 'em often falter.
Time may robe 'em in sackcloth coarse
  Or garb 'em in gorgeous splendor,
But whatever their lot, they keep one spot
  Down deep that is sweet an' tender.

We was speakin' of folks, jes' common folks,
  An' we come to this conclusion,
That one an' all, be they great or small,
  Will warm to a home allusion;
That under the skin an' the beaten hide
  They're kin in a real affection
For the joys they knew, when their years were
      few,
  An' the home of their recollection.

LITTLE MASTER MISCHIEVOUS

Little Master Mischievous, that's the name for
    you;
There's no better title that describes the things
    you do:
Into something all the while where you
    shouldn't be,
Prying into matters that are not for you to see;
Little Master Mischievous, order's overthrown
If your mother leaves you for a minute all
    alone.

Little Master Mischievous, opening every door,
Spilling books and papers round about the parlor
    floor,
Scratching all the tables and marring all the
    chairs,
Climbing where you shouldn't climb and tum-
    bling down the stairs.
How'd you get the ink well? We can never
    guess.
Now the rug is ruined; so's your little dress.

Little Master Mischievous, in the cookie jar,
Who has ever told you where the cookies are?
Now your sticky fingers smear the curtains
    white;
You have finger-printed everything in sight.

There's no use in scolding; when you smile that
    way
You can rob of terror every word we say.

Little Master Mischievous, that's the name for
    you;
There's no better title that describes the things
    you do:
Prying into corners, peering into nooks,
Tugging table covers, tearing costly books.
Little Master Mischievous, have your roguish
    way;
Time, I know, will stop you, soon enough some
    day.

OPPORTUNITY

So long as men shall be on earth
    There will be tasks for them to do,
Some way for them to show their worth;
    Each day shall bring its problems new.

And men shall dream of mightier deeds
    Than ever have been done before:
There always shall be human needs
    For men to work and struggle for.

THE SORROW TUGS

There's a lot of joy in the smiling world,
    there's plenty of morning sun,
And laughter and songs and dances, too, when-
    ever the day's work's done;
Full many an hour is a shining one, when
    viewed by itself apart,
But the golden threads in the warp of life are
    the sorrow tugs at your heart.

Oh, the fun is froth and it blows away, and
    many a joy's forgot,
And the pleasures come and the pleasures go,
    and memory holds them not;
But treasured ever you keep the pain that causes
    your tears to start,
For the sweetest hours are the ones that bring
    the sorrow tugs at your heart.

The lump in your throat and the little sigh when
    your baby trudged away
The very first time to the big red school — how
    long will their memory stay?
The fever days and the long black nights you
    watched as she troubled, slept,
And the joy you felt when she smiled once
    more — how long will that all be kept?

The glad hours live in a feeble way, but the sad
    ones never die.
His first long trousers caused a pang and you
    saw them with a sigh.
And the big still house when the boy and girl,
    unto youth and beauty grown,
To college went; will you e'er forget that first
    grim hour alone?

It seems as you look back over things, that all
    that you treasure dear
Is somehow blent in a wondrous way with a
    heart pang and a tear.
Though many a day is a joyous one when
    viewed by itself apart,
The golden threads in the warp of life are the
    sorrow tugs at your heart.

ONLY A DAD

Only a dad with a tired face,
Coming home from the daily race,
Bringing little of gold or fame
To show how well he has played the game;
But glad in his heart that his own rejoice
To see him come and to hear his voice.

Only a dad with a brood of four,
One of ten million men or more
Plodding along in the daily strife,
Bearing the whips and the scorns of life,
With never a whimper of pain or hate,
For the sake of those who at home await.

Only a dad, neither rich nor proud,
Merely one of the surging crowd,
Toiling, striving from day to day,
Facing whatever may come his way,
Silent whenever the harsh condemn,
And bearing it all for the love of them.

Only a dad but he gives his all,
To smooth the way for his children small,
Doing with courage stern and grim
The deeds that his father did for him.
This is the line that for him I pen:
Only a dad, but the best of men.

HARD KNOCKS

I'm not the man to say that failure's sweet,
  Nor tell a chap to laugh when things go
      wrong;
I know it hurts to have to take defeat
  An' no one likes to lose before a throng;
It isn't very pleasant not to win
  When you have done the very best you could;
But if you're down, get up an' buckle in —
  A lickin' often does a fellow good.

I've seen some chaps who never knew their
      power
  Until somebody knocked 'em to the floor;
I've known men who discovered in an hour
  A courage they had never shown before.
I've seen 'em rise from failure to the top
  By doin' things they hadn't understood
Before the day disaster made 'em drop —
  A lickin' often does a fellow good.

Success is not the teacher, wise an' true,
  That gruff old failure is, remember that;
She's much too apt to make a fool of you,
  Which isn't true of blows that knock you flat.
Hard knocks are painful things an' hard to bear,
  An' most of us would dodge 'em if we could;
There's something mighty broadening in care —
  A lickin' often does a fellow good.

SPRING IN THE TRENCHES

It's coming time for planting in that little patch
    of ground,
Where the lad and I made merry as he followed
    me around;
Now the sun is getting higher, and the skies
    above are blue,
And I'm hungry for the garden, and I wish the
    war was through.
      But it's tramp, tramp, tramp,
        And it's never look behind,
      And when you see a stranger's kids
        Pretend that you are blind.

The spring is coming back again, the birds
    begin to mate;
The skies are full of kindness, but the world is
    full of hate.
And it's I that should be bending now in peace
    above the soil
With laughing eyes and little hands about to
    bless the toil.
      But it's fight, fight, fight,
        And it's charge at double-quick;
      A soldier thinking thoughts of home
        Is one more soldier sick.

Last year I brought the bulbs to bloom and
      saw the roses bud;
This year I'm ankle deep in mire, and most of
      it is blood.
Last year the mother in the door was glad as
      she could be;
To-day her heart is full of pain, and mine is
      hurting me.
    But it's shoot, shoot, shoot,
    And when the bullets hiss,
    Don't let the tears fill up your eyes,
    For weeping soldiers miss.

Oh, who will tend the roses now and who will
      sow the seeds?
And who will do the heavy work the little
      garden needs?
And who will tell the lad of mine the things
      he wants to know,
And take his hand and lead him round the
      paths we used to go?
    For it's charge, charge, charge,
    And it's face the foe once more;
    Forget the things you love the most
    And keep your mind on gore.

FATHER

Used to wonder just why father
   Never had much time for play,
Used to wonder why he'd rather
   Work each minute of the day.
Used to wonder why he never
   Loafed along the road an' shirked;
Can't recall a time whenever
   Father played while others worked.

Father didn't dress in fashion,
   Sort of hated clothing new;
Style with him was not a passion;
   He had other things in view.
Boys are blind to much that's going
   On about 'em day by day,
And I had no way of knowing
   What became of father's pay.

All I knew was when I needed
   Shoes I got 'em on the spot;
Everything for which I pleaded,
   Somehow, father always got.
Wondered, season after season,
   Why he never took a rest,
And that *I* might be the reason
   Then I never even guessed.

Father set a store on knowledge;
  If he'd lived to have his way
He'd have sent me off to college
  And the bills been glad to pay.
That, I know, was his ambition:
  Now and then he used to say
He'd have done his earthly mission
  On my graduation day.

Saw his cheeks were getting paler,
  Didn't understand just why;
Saw his body growing frailer,
  Then at last I saw him die.
Rest had come! His tasks were ended,
  Calm was written on his brow;
Father's life was big and splendid,
  And I understand it now.

LADDIES

Show me the boy who **never** threw
  A stone at someone's **cat,**
Or never hurled a snowball swift
  At someone's high silk hat —
Who never ran away from school,
  To seek the swimming hole,
Or slyly from a neighbor's yard
  Green apples never stole —

Show me the boy who never broke
  A pane of window glass,
Who never disobeyed the sign
  That says: "Keep off the grass."
Who never did a thousand things,
  That grieve us sore to tell,
And I'll show you a little boy
  Who must be far from well.

THE LIVING BEAUTIES

I never knew, until they went,
How much their laughter really meant.
I never knew how much the place
Depended on each little face;
How barren home could be and drear
Without its living beauties here.

I never knew that chairs and books
Could wear such sad and solemn looks!
That rooms and halls could be at night
So still and drained of all delight.
This home is now but brick and board
Where bits of furniture are stored.

I used to think I loved each shelf
And room for what it was itself.
And once I thought each picture fine
Because I proudly called it mine.
But now I know they mean no more
Than art works hanging in a store.

Until they went away to roam
I never knew what made it home.
But I have learned that all is base,
However wonderful the place
And decked with costly treasures, rare,
Unless the living joys are there.

AT BREAKFAST TIME

My Pa he eats his breakfast in a funny sort of
    way:
We hardly ever see him at the first meal of the
    day.
Ma puts his food before him and he settles in
    his place
An' then he props the paper up and we can't
    see his face;
We hear him blow his coffee and we hear him
    chew his toast,
But it's for the morning paper that he seems
    to care the most.

Ma says that little children mighty grateful
    ought to be
To the folks that fixed the evening as the proper
    time for tea.
She says if meals were only served to people
    once a day,
An' that was in the morning just before Pa goes
    away,
We'd never know how father looked when he
    was in his place,
Coz he'd always have the morning paper stuck
    before his face.

He drinks his coffee steamin' hot, an' passes
Ma his cup
To have it filled a second time, an' never once
looks up.
He never has a word to say, but just sits there
an' reads,
An' when she sees his hand stuck out Ma gives
him what he needs.
She guesses what it is he wants, coz it's no use
to ask:
Pa's got to read his paper an' sometimes that's
quite a task.

One morning we had breakfast an' his features
we could see,
But his face was long an' solemn an' he didn't
speak to me,
An' we couldn't get him laughin' an' we couldn't
make him smile,
An' he said the toast was soggy an' the coffee
simply vile.
Then Ma said: "What's the matter? Why are
you so cross an' glum?"
An' Pa 'most took her head off coz the paper
didn't come.

CAN'T

Can't is the worst word that's written or
    spoken;
Doing more harm here than slander and lies;
On it is many a strong spirit broken,
    And with it many a good purpose dies.
It springs from the lips of the thoughtless each
    morning
    And robs us of courage we need through the
    day:
It rings in our ears like a timely-sent warning
    And laughs when we falter and fall by the
    way.

Can't is the father of feeble endeavor,
    The parent of terror and half-hearted work;
It weakens the efforts of artisans clever,
    And makes of the toiler an indolent shirk.
It poisons the soul of the man with a vision,
    It stifles in infancy many a plan;
It greets honest toiling with open derision
    And mocks at the hopes and the dreams of a
    man.

Can't is a word none should speak without
    blushing;
To utter it should be a symbol of shame;
Ambition and courage it daily is crushing;

It blights a man's purpose and shortens his
    aim.
Despise it with all of your hatred of error;
    Refuse it the lodgment it seeks in your brain;
Arm against it as a creature of terror,
    And all that you dream of you some day shall
    gain.

Can't is the word that is foe to ambition,
    An enemy ambushed to shatter your will;
Its prey is forever the man with a mission
    And bows but to courage and patience and
    skill.
Hate it, with hatred that's deep and undying,
    For once it is welcomed 'twill break any
    man;
Whatever the goal you are seeking, keep trying
    And answer this demon by saying: " I *can*."

JAMES WHITCOMB RILEY

Written July 22, 1916, when the world lost its "Poet of Childhood."

There must be great rejoicin' on the Golden
    Shore to-day,
An' the big an' little angels must be feelin'
    mighty gay:
Could we look beyond the curtain now I fancy
    we should see
Old Aunt Mary waitin', smilin', for the coming
    that's to be,
An' Little Orphant Annie an' the whole excited
    pack
Dancin' up an' down an' shoutin': "Mr. Riley's
    comin' back!"

There's a heap o' real sadness in this good old
    world to-day;
There are lumpy throats this morning now that
    Riley's gone away;
There's a voice now stilled forever that in
    sweetness only spoke
An' whispered words of courage with a faith that
    never broke.
There is much of joy and laughter that we
    mortals here will lack,
But the angels must be happy now that Riley's
    comin' back.

The world was gettin' dreary, there was too
    much sigh an' frown
In this vale o' mortal strivin', so God sent Jim
    Riley down,
An' He said: "Go there an' cheer 'em in your
    good old-fashioned way,
With your songs of tender sweetness, but don't
    make your plans to stay,
Coz you're needed up in Heaven. I am lendin'
    you to men
Just to help 'em with your music, but I'll want
    you back again."

An' Riley came, an' mortals heard the music of
    his voice
An' they caught his songs o' beauty an' they
    started to rejoice;
An' they leaned on him in sorrow, an' they
    shared with him their joys,
An' they walked with him the pathways that
    they knew when they were boys.
But the heavenly angels missed him, missed his
    tender, gentle knack
Of makin' people happy, an' they wanted Riley
    back.

There must be great rejoicin' on the streets of
    Heaven to-day
An' all the angel children must be troopin'
    down the way,

Singin' heavenly songs of welcome an' pre-
    parin' now to greet
The soul that God had tinctured with an ever-
    lasting sweet;
The world is robed in sadness an' is draped in
    sombre black;
But joy must reign in Heaven now that Riley's
    comin' back.

RESULTS AND ROSES

The man who wants a garden fair,
    Or small or very big,
With flowers growing here and there,
    Must bend his back and dig.

The things are mighty few on earth
    That wishes can attain.
Whate'er we want of any worth
    We've got to work to gain.

It matters not what goal you seek
    Its secret here reposes:
You've got to dig from week to week
    To get Results or Roses.

THE OTHER FELLOW

Are you fond of your wife and your children
     fair?
  So is the other fellow.
Do you crave pleasures for them to share?
  So does the other fellow.
Does your heart rejoice when your own are
     glad?
And are you troubled when they are sad?
Well, it's that way, too, in this life, my lad,
  That way with the other fellow.

Do you want the best for your own to know?
  So does the other fellow.
Do you stoop to kiss them before you go?
  So does the other fellow.
When your baby lies on a fevered bed,
Does your heart run cold with a silent dread?
Well, it's that way, too, where all mortals tread—
  That way with the other fellow.

Does it hurt when they want what you cannot
     buy?
  It does with the other fellow.
Do you for their comfort yourself deny?
  So does the other fellow.
Would you wail aloud if your babe should die
For the lack of care you could not supply?
Well, it's that way, too, as he travels by,
  That way with the other fellow.

OUR DUTY TO OUR FLAG

Less hate and greed
Is what we need
And more of service true;
More men to love
The flag above
And keep it first in view.

Less boast and brag
About the flag,
More faith in what it means:
More heads erect,
More self-respect,
Less talk of war machines.

The time to fight
To keep it bright
Is not along the way,
Nor 'cross the foam,
But here at home
Within ourselves — to-day.

'Tis we must love
That flag above
With all our might and main;
For from our hands,
Not distant lands,
Shall come dishonor's stain.

If that flag be
Dishonored, we
Have done it, not the foe;
If it shall fall
We first of all
Shall be to strike a blow.

THE HUNTER

Cheek that is tanned to the wind of the north,
    Body that jests at the bite of the cold,
Limbs that are eager and strong to go forth
    Into the wilds and the ways of the bold;
Red blood that pulses and throbs in the veins,
    Ears that love silences better than noise;
Strength of the forest and health of the plains:
    These the rewards that the hunter enjoys.

Forests were ever the cradles of men;
    Manhood is born of a kinship with trees.
Whence shall come brave hearts and stout
        muscles, when
    Woods have made way for our cities of ease?
Oh, do you wonder that stalwarts return
    Yearly to hark to the whispering oaks?
'Tis for the brave days of old that they yearn:
    These are the splendors the hunter invokes.

IT'S SEPTEMBER

It's September, and the orchards are afire with
    red and gold,
And the nights with dew are heavy, and the
    morning's sharp with cold;
Now the garden's at its gayest with the salvia
    blazing red
And the good old-fashioned asters laughing
    at us from their bed;
Once again in shoes and stockings are the chil-
    dren's little feet,
And the dog now does his snoozing on the
    bright side of the street.

It's September, and the cornstalks are as high
    as they will go,
And the red cheeks of the apples everywhere
    begin to show;
Now the supper's scarcely over ere the dark-
    ness settles down
And the moon looms big and yellow at the
    edges of the town;
Oh, it's good to see the children, when their
    little prayers are said,
Duck beneath the patchwork covers when they
    tumble into bed.

It's September, and a calmness and a sweetness
    seem to fall
Over everything that's living, just as though it
    hears the call
Of Old Winter, trudging slowly, with his pack
    of ice and snow,
In the distance over yonder, and it somehow
    seems as though
Every tiny little blossom wants to look its very
    best
When the frost shall bite its petals and it droops
    away to rest.

It's September! It's the fullness and the ripe-
    ness of the year;
All the work of earth is finished, or the final
    tasks are near,
But there is no doleful wailing; every living
    thing that grows,
For the end that is approaching wears the
    finest garb it knows.
And I pray that I may proudly hold my head
    up high and smile
When I come to my September in the golden
    afterwhile.

HOW DO YOU TACKLE YOUR WORK?

How do you tackle your work each day?
  Are you scared of the job you find?
Do you grapple the task that comes your way
  With a confident, easy mind?
Do you stand right up to the work ahead
  Or fearfully pause to view it?
Do you start to toil with a sense of dread
  Or feel that you're going to do it?

You can do as much as you think you can,
  But you'll never accomplish more;
If you're afraid of yourself, young man,
  There's little for you in store.
For failure comes from the inside first,
  It's there if we only knew it,
And you can win, though you face the worst,
  If you feel that you're going to do it.

Success! It's found in the soul of you,
  And not in the realm of luck!
The world will furnish the work to do,
  But you must provide the pluck.
You can do whatever you think you can,
  It's all in the way you view it.
It's all in the start that you make, young man:
  You must feel that you're going to do it.

How do you tackle your work each day?
　　With confidence clear, or dread?
What to yourself do you stop and say
　　When a new task lies ahead?
What is the thought that is in your mind?
　　Is fear ever running through it?
If so, just tackle the next you find
　　By thinking you're going to do it.

LIFE

Life is a gift to be used every day,
Not to be smothered and hidden away;
It isn't a thing to be stored in the chest
Where you gather your keepsakes and treasure
　　　your best;
It isn't a joy to be sipped now and then
And promptly put back in a dark place again.

Life is a gift that the humblest may boast of
And one that the humblest may well make the
　　　most of.
Get out and live it each hour of the day,
Wear it and use it as much as you may;
Don't keep it in niches and corners and grooves,
You'll find that in service its beauty improves.

STORY TELLING

Most every night when they're in bed,
And both their little prayers have said,
They shout for me to come upstairs
And tell them tales of grizzly bears,
And Indians and gypsies bold,
And eagles with the claws that hold
A baby's weight, and fairy sprites
That roam the woods on starry nights.

And I must illustrate these tales,
Must imitate the northern gales
That toss the Indian's canoe,
And show the way he paddles, too.
If in the story comes a bear,
I have to pause and sniff the air
And show the way he climbs the trees
To steal the honey from the bees.

And then I buzz like angry bees
And sting him on his nose and knees
And howl in pain, till mother cries:
" That pair will never shut their eyes,
While all that noise up there you make;
You're simply keeping them awake."
And then they whisper: " Just one more,"
And once again I'm forced to roar.

New stories every night they ask,
And that is not an easy task;
I have to be so many things,
The frog that croaks, the lark that sings,
The cunning fox, the frightened hen;
But just last night they stumped me, when
They wanted me to twist and squirm
And imitate an angle worm.

At last they tumble off to sleep,
And softly from their room I creep
And brush and comb the shock of hair
I tossed about to be a bear.
Then mother says: " Well, I should say
You're just as much a child as they."
But you can bet I'll not resign
That story telling job of mine.

CANNING TIME

There's a wondrous smell of spices
     In the kitchen,
      Most bewitchin';
There are fruits cut into slices
That just set the palate itchin';
There's the sound of spoon on platter
And the rattle and the clatter;
And a bunch of kids are hastin'
To the splendid joy of tastin':
It's the fragrant time of year
When fruit-cannin' days are here.

There's a good wife gayly smilin'
     And perspirin'
      Some, and tirin';
And while jar on jar she's pilin'
And the necks o' them she's wirin'
I'm a-sittin' here an' dreamin'
Of the kettles that are steamin',
And the cares that have been troublin'
All have vanished in the bubblin'.
I am happy that I'm here
At the cannin' time of year.

Lord, I'm sorry for the feller
     That is missin'
      All the hissin'
Of the juices, red and yeller,

And can never sit and listen
To the rattle and the clatter
Of the sound of spoon on platter.
I am sorry for the single,
For they miss the thrill and tingle
Of the splendid time of year
When the cannin' days are here.

THE DULL ROAD

It's the dull road that leads to the gay road
  The practice that leads to success;
The work road that leads to the play road;
  It is trouble that breeds happiness.

It's the hard work and merciless grinding
  That purchases glory and fame;
It's repeatedly doing, nor minding
  The drudgery drear of the game.

It's the passing up glamor or pleasure
  For the sake of the skill we may gain,
And in giving up comfort or leisure
  For the joy that we hope to attain.

It's the hard road of trying and learning,
  Of toiling, uncheered and alone,
That wins us the prizes worth earning,
  And leads us to goals we would own.

THE APPLE TREE

When an apple tree is ready for the world to
    come and eat,
There isn't any structure in the land that's
    " got it beat."
There's nothing man has builded with the
    beauty or the charm
That can touch the simple grandeur of the
    monarch of the farm.
There's never any picture from a human
    being's brush
That has ever caught the redness of a single
    apple's blush.

When an apple tree's in blossom it is glorious
    to see,
But that's just a hint, at springtime, of the
    better things to be;
That is just a fairy promise from the Great
    Magician's wand
Of the wonders and the splendors that are
    waiting just beyond
The distant edge of summer; just a forecast
    of the treat
When the apple tree is ready for the world
    to come and eat.

Architects of splendid vision long have labored
    on the earth,
And have raised their dreams in marble and
    we've marveled at their worth;
Long the spires of costly churches have looked
    upward at the sky;
Rich in promise and in the beauty, they have
    cheered the passer-by.
But I'm sure there's nothing finer for the eye
    of man to meet
Than an apple tree that's ready for the world
    to come and eat.

There's the promise of the apples, red and
    gleaming in the sun,
Like the medals worn by mortals as rewards
    for labors done;
And the big arms stretched wide open, with a
    welcome warm and true
In a way that sets you thinking it's intended
    just for you.
There is nothing with a beauty so entrancing,
    so complete,
As an apple tree that's ready for the world to
    come and eat.

THE HOME-TOWN

Some folks leave home for money
   And some leave home for fame,
Some seek skies always sunny,
   And some depart in shame.
I care not what the reason
   Men travel east or west,
Or what the month or season —
   The home-town is the best.

The home-town is the glad town
   Where something real abides;
'Tis not the money-mad town
   That all its spirit hides.
Though strangers scoff and flout it
   And even jeer its name,
It has a charm about it
   No other town can claim.

The home-town skies seem bluer
   Than skies that stretch away.
The home-town friends seem truer
   And kinder through the day;
And whether glum or cheery
   Light-hearted or depressed,
Or struggle-fit or weary,
   I like the home-town best.

Let him who will, go wander
  To distant towns to live,
Of some things I am fonder
  Than all they have to give.
The gold of distant places
  Could not repay me quite
For those familiar faces
  That keep the home-town bright.

TAKE HOME A SMILE

Take home a smile; forget the petty cares,
The dull, grim grind of all the day's affairs;
The day is done, come be yourself awhile:
To-night, to those who wait, take home a smile.

Take home a smile; don't scatter grief and gloom
Where laughter and light hearts should always
        bloom;
What though you've traveled many a dusty mile,
Footsore and weary, still take home a smile.

Take home a smile — it is not much to do,
But much it means to them who wait for you;
You can be brave for such a little while;
The day of doubt is done — take home a smile

COURAGE

Courage isn't a brilliant dash,
A daring deed in a moment's flash;
It isn't an instantaneous thing
Born of despair with a sudden spring
It isn't a creature of flickered hope
Or the final tug at a slipping rope;
But it's something deep in the soul of man
That is working always to serve some plan.

Courage isn't the last resort
In the work of life or the game of sport;
It isn't a thing that a man can call
At some future time when he's apt to fall;
If he hasn't it now, he will have it not
When the strain is great and the pace is hot.
For who would strive for a distant goal
Must always have courage within his soul.

Courage isn't a dazzling light
That flashes and passes away from sight;
It's a slow, unwavering, ingrained trait
With the patience to work and the strength to
        wait.
It's part of a man when his skies are blue,
It's part of him when he has work to do.
The brave man never is freed of it.
He has it when there is no need of it.

Courage was never designed for show;
It isn't a thing that can come and go;
It's written in victory and defeat
And every trial a man may meet.
It's part of his hours, his days and his years,
Back of his smiles and behind his tears.
Courage is more than a daring deed:
It's the breath of life and a strong man's creed.

GREATNESS

We can be great by helping one another;
  We can be loved for very simple deeds:
Who has the grateful mention of a brother
  Has really all the honor that he needs.

We can be famous for our works of kindness —
  Fame is not born alone of strength or skill;
It sometimes comes from deafness and from
      blindness
  To petty words and faults, and loving still.

We can be rich in gentle smiles and sunny:
  A jeweled soul exceeds a royal crown.
The richest men sometimes have little money,
  And Croesus oft's the poorest man in town.

THE EPICURE

I've sipped a rich man's sparkling wine,
   His silverware I've handled.
I've placed these battered legs of mine
   'Neath tables gayly candled.
I dine on rare and costly fare
   Whene'er good fortune lets me,
But there's no meal that can compare
   With those the missus gets me.

I've had your steaks three inches thick
   With all your Sam Ward trimming,
I've had the breast of milk-fed chick
   In luscious gravy swimming.
To dine in swell café or club
   But irritates and frets me;
Give me the plain and wholesome grub —
   The grub the missus gets me.

Two kiddies smiling at the board,
   The cook right at the table,
The four of us, a hungry horde,
   To beat that none is able.
A big meat pie, with flaky crust!
   'Tis then that joy besets me;
Oh, I could eat until I "bust,"
   Those meals the missus gets me.

THE GENTLE GARDENER

I'd like to leave but daffodills to mark my little
  way,
To leave but tulips red and white behind me as
  I stray;
I'd like to pass away from earth and feel I'd
  left behind
But roses and forget-me-nots for all who come
  to find.

I'd like to sow the barren spots with all the
  flowers of earth,
To leave a path where those who come should
  find but gentle mirth;
And when at last I'm called upon to join the
  heavenly throng
I'd like to feel along my way I'd left no sign
  of wrong.

And yet the cares are many and the hours of
  toil are few;
There is not time enough on earth for all I'd
  like to do;
But, having lived and having toiled, I'd like the
  world to find
Some little touch of beauty that my soul had
  left behind.

THE FINEST AGE

When he was only nine months old,
  And plump and round and pink of cheek,
A joy to tickle and to hold,
  Before he'd even learned to speak,
His gentle mother used to say:
  "It is too bad that he must grow.
If I could only have my way
  His baby ways we'd always know."

And then the year was turned, and he
  Began to toddle round the floor
And name the things that he could see
  And soil the dresses that he wore.
Then many a night she whispered low:
  "Our baby now is such a joy
I hate to think that he must grow
  To be a wild and heedless boy."

But on he went and sweeter grew,
  And then his mother, I recall,
Wished she could keep him always two,
  For that's the finest age of all.
She thought the selfsame thing at three,
  And now that he is four, she sighs
To think he cannot always be
  The youngster with the laughing eyes.

Oh, little boy, my wish is not
   Always to keep you four years old.
Each night I stand beside your cot
   And think of what the years may hold;
And looking down on you I pray
   That when we've lost our baby small,
The mother of our man will say
   "This is the finest age of all."

SUCCESS AND FAILURE

I do not think all failure's undeserved,
   And all success is merely someone's luck;
Some men are down because they were unnerved,
   And some are up because they kept their pluck.
Some men are down because they chose to shirk;
Some men are high because they did their work.

I do not think that all the poor are good,
   That riches are the uniform of shame;
The beggar might have conquered if he would,
   And that he begs, the world is not to blame.
Misfortune is not all that comes to mar;
Most men, themselves, have shaped the things
      they are.

CARE-FREE YOUTH

The skies are blue and the sun is out and the
    grass is green and soft
And the old charm's back in the apple tree
    and it calls a boy aloft;
And the same low voice that the old don't hear,
    but the care-free youngsters do,
Is calling them to the fields and streams and
    the joys that once I knew.
And if youth be wild desire for play and care
    is the mark of men,
Beneath the skin that Time has tanned I'm a
    madcap youngster then.

Far richer than king with his crown of gold and
    his heavy weight of care
Is the sunburned boy with his stone-bruised feet
    and his tousled shock of hair;
For the king can hear but the cry of hate or the
    sickly sound of praise,
And lost to him are the voices sweet that called
    in his boyhood days.
Far better than ruler, with pomp and power
    and riches, is it to be
The urchin gay in his tattered clothes that is
    climbing the apple tree.

Oh, once I heard all the calls that come to the
    quick, glad ears of boys,

And a certain spot on the river bank told me of
    its many joys,
And certain fields and certain trees were loyal
    friends to me,
And I knew the birds, and I owned a dog, and
    we both could hear and see.
Oh, never from tongues of men have dropped
    such messages wholly glad
As the things that live in the great outdoors
    once told to a little lad.

And I'm sorry for him who cannot hear what
    the tall trees have to say,
Who is deaf to the call of a running stream
    and the lanes that lead to play.
The boy that shins up the faithful elm or
    sprawls on a river bank
Is more richly blessed with the joys of life than
    any old man of rank.
For youth is the golden time of life, and this
    battered old heart of mine
Beats fast to the march of its old-time joys,
    when the sun begins to shine.

MY PAW SAID SO

Foxes can talk if you know how to listen,
    My Paw said so.
Owls have big eyes that sparkle an' glisten,
    My Paw said so.
Bears can turn flip-flaps an' climb ellum trees,
An' steal all the honey away from the bees,
An' they never mind winter becoz they don't
    freeze;
    My Paw said so.

Girls is a-scared of a snake, but boys ain't,
    My Paw said so.
They holler an' run; an' sometimes they faint,
    My Paw said so.
But boys would be 'shamed to be frightened
    that way
When all that the snake wants to do is to play:
You've got to believe every word that I say,
    My Paw said so.

Wolves ain't so bad if you treat 'em all right,
    My Paw said so.
They're as fond of a game as they are of a fight,
    My Paw said so.
An' all of the animals found in the wood
Ain't always ferocious. Most times they are
    good.

The trouble is mostly they're misunderstood,
    My Paw said so.
You can think what you like, but I stick to it
        when
    My Paw said so.
An' I'll keep right on sayin', again an' again,
    My Paw said so.
Maybe foxes don't talk to such people as you,
An' bears never show you the tricks they can do,
But I know that the stories I'm tellin' are true
    My Paw said so.

LIFE'S TESTS

If never a sorrow came to us, and never a care
        we knew;
If every hope were realized, and every dream
        came true;
If only joy were found on earth, and no one
        ever sighed,
And never a friend proved false to us, and never
        a loved one died,
And never a burden bore us down, soul-sick and
        weary, too,
We'd yearn for tests to prove our worth and
        tasks for us to do.

THE PEACEFUL WARRIORS

Let others sing their songs of war
  And chant their hymns of splendid death,
Let others praise the soldiers' ways
  And hail the cannon's flaming breath.
Let others sing of Glory's fields
  Where blood for Victory is paid,
I choose to sing some simple thing
  To those who wield not gun or blade —
  The peaceful warriors of trade.

Let others choose the deeds of war
  For symbols of our nation's skill,
The blood-red coat, the rattling throat,
  The regiment that charged the hill,
The boy who died to serve the flag,
  Who heard the order and obeyed,
But leave to me the gallantry
  Of those who labor unafraid —
  The peaceful warriors of trade.

Aye, let me sing the splendid deeds
  Of those who toil to serve mankind,
The men who break old ways and make
  New paths for those who come behind.
The young who war with customs old
  And face their problems, unafraid,
Who think and plan to lift for man
  The burden that on him is laid —
  The splendid warriors of trade.

I sing of battles with disease
   And victories o'er death and pain,
Of ships that fly the summer sky,
   And glorious deeds of strength and brain.
The call for help that rings through space
   By which a vessel's course is stayed,
Thrills me far more than fields of gore,
   Or heroes decked in golden braid —
   I sing the warriors of trade.

FAILURES

'Tis better to have tried in vain,
   Sincerely striving for a goal,
Than to have lived upon the plain
   An idle and a timid soul.

'Tis better to have fought and spent
   Your courage, missing all applause,
Than to have lived in smug content
   And never ventured for a cause.

For he who tries and fails may be
   The founder of a better day;
Though never his the victory,
   From him shall others learn the way.

RAISIN PIE

There's a heap of pent-up goodness in the yellow
    bantam corn,
And I sort o' like to linger round a berry patch
    at morn;
Oh, the Lord has set our table with a stock o'
    things to eat
An' there's just enough o' bitter in the blend
    to cut the sweet,
But I run the whole list over, an' it seems
    somehow that I
Find the keenest sort o' pleasure in a chunk
    o' raisin pie.

There are pies that start the water circulatin' in
    the mouth;
There are pies that wear the flavor of the warm
    an' sunny south;
Some with oriental spices spur the drowsy appe-
    tite
An' just fill a fellow's being with a thrill o'
    real delight;
But for downright solid goodness that comes
    drippin' from the sky
There is nothing quite the equal of a chunk o'
    raisin pie.

I'm admittin' tastes are diff'runt, I'm not settin'
    up myself

As the judge an' final critic of the good things
 on the shelf.
I'm just sort o' payin' tribute to a simple joy on
 earth,
Sort o' feebly testifyin' to its lasting charm an'
 worth,
An' I'll hold to this conclusion till it comes my
 time to die,
That there's no dessert that's finer than a chunk
 o' raisin pie.

PREPAREDNESS

Right must not live in idleness,
 Nor dwell in smug content;
It must be strong, against the throng
 Of foes, on evil bent.

Justice must not a weakling be
 But it must guard its own,
And live each day, that none can say
 Justice is overthrown.

Peace, the sweet glory of the world,
 Faces a duty, too;
Death is her fate, leaves she one gate
 For war to enter through.

THE READY ARTISTS

The green is in the meadow and the blue is in
    the sky,
And all of Nature's artists have their colors
    handy by;
With a few days bright with sunshine and a
    few nights free from frost
They will start to splash their colors quite
    regardless of the cost.
There's an artist waiting ready at each bleak
    and dismal spot
To paint the flashing tulip or the meek forget-
    me-not.

May is lurking in the distance and her lap is
    filled with flowers,
And the choicest of her blossoms very shortly
    will be ours.
There is not a lane so dreary or a field so dark
    with gloom
But that soon will be resplendent with its little
    touch of bloom.
There's an artist keen and eager to make beau-
    tiful each scene
And remove with colors gorgeous every trace of
    of what has been.

Oh, the world is now in mourning; round about
us all are spread
The ruins and the symbols of the winter that
is dead.
But the bleak and barren picture very shortly
now will pass,
For the halls of life are ready for their velvet
rugs of grass;
And the painters now are waiting with their
magic to replace
This dullness with a beauty that no mortal hand
can trace.

The green is in the meadow and the blue is in
the sky;
The chill of death is passing, life will shortly
greet the eye.
We shall revel soon in colors only Nature's
artists make
And the humblest plant that's sleeping unto
beauty shall awake.
For there's not a leaf forgotten, not a twig
neglected there,
And the tiniest of pansies shall the royal purple
wear.

THE HAPPIEST DAYS

You do not know it, little man,
In your summer coat of tan
And your legs bereft of hose
And your peeling, sunburned nose,
With a stone bruise on your toe,
Almost limping as you go
Running on your way to play
Through another summer day,
Friend of birds and streams and trees,
That your happiest days are these.

Little do you think to-day,
As you hurry to your play,
That a lot of us, grown old
In the chase for fame and gold,
Watch you as you pass along
Gayly whistling bits of song,
And in envy sit and dream
Of a long-neglected stream,
Where long buried are the joys
We possessed when we were boys.

Little chap, you cannot guess
All your sum of happiness;
Little value do you place
On your sunburned freckled face;

And if some shrewd fairy came
Offering sums of gold and fame
For your summer days of play,
You would barter them away
And believe that you had made
There and then a clever trade.

Time was we were boys like you,
Bare of foot and sunburned, too,
And, like you, we never guessed
All the riches we possessed;
We'd have traded them back then
For the hollow joys of men;
We'd have given them all to be
Rich and wise and forty-three.
For life never teaches boys
Just how precious are their joys.

Youth has fled and we are old.
Some of us have fame and gold;
Some of us are sorely scarred,
For the way of age is hard;
And we envy, little man,
You your splendid coat of tan,
Envy you your treasures rare,
Hours of joy beyond compare;
For we know, by teaching stern,
All that some day you must learn.

THE REAL BAIT

To gentle ways I am inclined;
    I have no wish to kill.
To creatures dumb I would be kind;
    I like them all, but still
Right now I think I'd like to be
    Beside some rippling brook,
And grab a worm I'd brought with me
    And slip him on a hook.

I'd like to put my hand once more
    Into a rusty can
And turn those squirmy creatures o'er
    Like nuggets in a pan;
And for a big one, once again,
    With eager eyes I'd look,
As did a boy I knew, and then
    Impale it on a hook.

I've had my share of fishing joy,
    I've fished with patent bait,
With chub and minnow, but the boy
    Is lord of sport's estate.
And no such pleasure comes to man
    So rare as when he took
A worm from a tomato can
    And slipped it on a hook.

I'd like to gaze with glowing eyes
  Upon that precious bait,
To view each fat worm as a prize
  To be accounted great.
And though I've passed from boyhood's term,
  And opened age's book,
I still would like to put a worm
  That wriggled on a hook.

TRUE NOBILITY

Who does his task from day to day
And meets whatever comes his way,
Believing God has willed it so,
Has found real greatness here below.

Who guards his post, no matter where,
Believing God must need him there,
Although but lowly toil it be,
Has risen to nobility.

For great and low there's but one test:
'Tis that each man shall do his best.
Who works with all the strength he can
Shall never die in debt to man.

THE SULKERS

The world's too busy now to pause
To listen to a whiner's cause;
It has no time to stop and pet
The sulker in a peevish fret,
Who wails he'll neither work nor play
Because things haven't gone his way.

The world keeps plodding right along
And gives its favors right or wrong
To all who have the grit to work
Regardless of the fool or shirk.
The world says this to every man:
" Go out and do the best you can."

The world's too busy to implore
The beaten one to try once more;
'Twill help him if he wants to rise,
And boost him if he bravely tries,
And shows determination grim;
But it won't stop to baby him.

The world is occupied with men
Who fall but quickly rise again;
But those who whine because they're hit
And step aside to sulk a bit
Are doomed some day to wake and find
The world has left them far behind.

PURPOSE

Not for the sake of the gold,
　Not for the sake of the fame,
Not for the prize would I hold
　Any ambition or aim:
I would be brave and be true
Just for the good I can do.

I would be useful on earth,
　Serving some purpose or cause,
Doing some labor of worth,
　Giving no thought to applause.
Thinking less of the gold or the fame
Than the joy and the thrill of the game.

Medals their brightness may lose,
　Fame be forgotten or fade,
Any reward we may choose
　Leaves the account still unpaid.
But little real happiness lies
In fighting alone for a prize.

Give me the thrill of the task,
　The joy of the battle and strife,
Of being of use, and I'll ask
　No greater reward from this life.
Better than fame or applause
Is striving to further a cause.

I've told about the times that Ma can't find
    her pocketbook,
And how we have to hustle round for it to help
    her look,
But there's another care we know that often
    comes our way,
I guess it happens easily a dozen times a day.
It starts when first the postman through the
    door a letter passes,
And Ma says: "Goodness gracious me! Wher-
    ever are my glasses?"

We hunt 'em on the mantelpiece an' by the
    kitchen sink,
Until Ma says: "Now, children, stop, an' give
    me time to think
Just when it was I used 'em last an' just
    exactly where.
Yes, now I know — the dining room. I'm sure
    you'll find 'em there."
We even look behind the clock, we busy boys
    an' lasses,
Until somebody runs across Ma's missing pair of
    glasses.

We've found 'em in the Bible, an' we've found
  'em in the flour,
We've found 'em in the sugar bowl, an' once
  we looked an hour
Before we came across 'em in the padding of
  her chair;
An' many a time we've found 'em in the topknot
  of her hair.
It's a search that ruins order an' the home com-
  pletely wrecks,
For there's no place where you may not find
  poor Ma's elusive specs.

But we're mighty glad, I tell you, that the
  duty's ours to do,
An' we hope to hunt those glasses till our time
  of life is through;
It's a little bit of service that is joyous in its
  thrill,
It's a task that calls us daily an' we hope it
  always will.
Rich or poor, the saddest mortals of all the
  joyless masses
Are the ones who have no mother dear to lose
  her reading glasses.

THE PRINCESS PAT'S

Written when the Canadian regiment, known as the "Princess Pat's," left for the front.

A touch of the plain and the prairie,
  A bit of the Motherland, too;
A strain of the fur-trapper wary,
  A blend of the old and the new;
A bit of the pioneer splendor
  That opened the wilderness' flats,
A touch of the home-lover, tender,
  You'll find in the boys they call Pat's.

The glory and grace of the maple,
  The strength that is born of the wheat,
The pride of a stock that is staple,
  The bronze of a midsummer heat;
A blending of wisdom and daring,
  The best of a new land, and that's
The regiment gallantly bearing
  The neat little title of Pat's.

A bit of the man who has neighbored
  With mountains and forests and streams,
A touch of the man who has labored
  To model and fashion his dreams;
The strength of an age of clean living,
  Of right-minded fatherly chats,
The best that a land could be giving
  Is there in the breasts of the Pat's.

BE A FRIEND

Be a friend. You don't need money:
Just a disposition sunny;
Just the wish to help another
Get along some way or other;
Just a kindly hand extended
Out to one who's unbefriended;
Just the·will to give or lend,
This will make you someone's friend.

Be a friend. You don't need glory.
Friendship is a simple story.
Pass by trifling errors blindly,
Gaze on honest effort kindly,
Cheer the youth who's bravely trying,
Pity him who's sadly sighing;
Just a little labor spend
On the duties of a friend.

Be a friend. The pay is bigger
(Though not written by a figure)
Than is earned by people clever
In what's merely self-endeavor.
You'll have friends instead of neighbors
For the profits of your labors;
You'll be richer in the end
Than a prince, if you're a friend.

THANKSGIVING

Thankful for the glory of the old Red, White
    and Blue,
For the spirit of America that still is staunch
    and true,
For the laughter of our children and the sun-
    light in their eyes,
And the joy of radiant mothers and their even-
    ing lullabies;
And thankful that our harvests wear no taint
    of blood to-day,
But were sown and reaped by toilers who were
    light of heart and gay.

Thankful for the riches that are ours to claim
    and keep,
The joy of honest labor and the boon of happy
    sleep,
For each little family circle where there is no
    empty chair
Save where God has sent the sorrow for the
    loving hearts to bear;
And thankful for the loyal souls and brave
    hearts of the past
Who builded that contentment should be with
    us to the last.

Thankful for the plenty that our peaceful land
    has blessed,
For the rising sun that beckons every man to
    do his best,
For the goal that lies before him and the promise
    when he sows
That his hand shall reap the harvest, undisturbed
    by cruel foes;
For the flaming torch of justice, symbolizing
    as it burns:
Here none may rob the toiler of the prize he
    fairly earns.

To-day our thanks we're giving for the riches
    that are ours,
For the red fruits of the orchards and the per-
    fume of the flowers,
For our homes with laughter ringing and our
    hearthfires blazing bright,
For our land of peace and plenty and our land
    of truth and right;
And we're thankful for the glory of the old
    Red, White and Blue,
For the spirit of our fathers and a manhood
    that is true.

MA AND HER CHECK BOOK

Ma has a dandy little book that's full of narrow
    slips,
An' when she wants to pay a bill a page from
    it she rips;
She just writes in the dollars and the cents and
    signs her name
An' that's as good as money, though it doesn't
    lock the same.
When she wants another bonnet or some
    feathers for her neck,
She promptly goes an' gets 'em, an' she writes
    another check.
I don't just understand it, but I know she
    sputters when
Pa says to her at supper: "Well! You're
    overdrawn again!"

Ma's not a business woman, she is much too
    kind of heart
To squabble over pennies or to play a selfish
    part,
An' when someone asks for money, she's not
    one to stop an' think
Of a little piece of paper an' the cost of pen
    an' ink.

She just tells him very sweetly if he'll only
    wait a bit
An' be seated in the parlor, she will write a
    check for it.
She can write one out for twenty just as easily
    as ten,
An' forgets that Pa may grumble: "Well,
    you're overdrawn again!"

Pa says it looks as though he'll have to start in
    workin' nights
To gather in the money for the checks that
    mother writes.
He says that every morning when he's sum-
    moned to the phone,
He's afraid the bank is calling to make mother's
    shortage known.
He tells his friends if ever anything our fortune
    wrecks
They can trace it to the moment mother started
    writing checks.
He's got so that he trembles when he sees her
    fountain pen
An' he mutters: "Do be careful! You'll be
    overdrawn again!"

THE FISHING CURE

There's nothing that builds up a toil-weary soul
  Like a day on a stream,
Back on the banks of the old fishing hole
  Where a fellow can dream.
There's nothing so good for a man as to flee
  From the city and lie
Full length in the shade of a whispering tree
  And gaze at the sky.

Out there where the strife and the greed are
    forgot
  And the struggle for pelf,
A man can get rid of each taint and each spot
  And clean up himself;
He can be what he wanted to be when a boy,
  If only in dreams;
And revel once more in the depths of a joy
  That's as real as it seems.

The things that he hates never follow him
    there —
  The jar of the street,
The rivalries petty, the struggling unfair —
  For the open is sweet.
In purity's realm he can rest and be clean,
  Be he humble or great,
And as peaceful his soul may become as the
    scene
  That his eyes contemplate.

It is good for the world that men hunger to go
  To the banks of a stream,
And weary of sham and of pomp and of show
  They have somewhere to dream.
For this life would be dreary and sordid and base
  Did they not now and then
Seek refreshment and calm in God's wide, open
    space
  And come back to be men.

THE HAPPY SLOW THINKER

Full many a time a thought has come
  That had a bitter meaning in it.
And in the conversation's hum
  I lost it ere I could begin it.

I've had it on my tongue to spring
  Some poisoned quip that I thought clever;
Then something happened and the sting
  Unuttered went, and died forever.

A lot of bitter thoughts I've had
  To silence fellows and to flay 'em,
But next day always I've been glad
  I wasn't quick enough to say 'em.

OUT-OF-DOORS

The kids are out-of-doors once more;
The heavy leggins that they wore,
The winter caps that covered ears
Are put away, and no more tears
Are shed because they cannot go
Until they're bundled up just so.
No more she wonders when they're gone
If they have put their rubbers on;
No longer are they hourly told
To guard themselves against a cold;
Bareheaded now they romp and run
Warmed only by the kindly sun.

She's put their heavy clothes away
And turned the children out to play,
And all the morning long they race
Like madcaps round about the place.
The robins on the fences sing
A gayer song of welcoming,
And seem as though they had a share
In all the fun they're having there.
The wrens and sparrows twitter, too,
A louder and a noisier crew,
As though it pleased them all to see
The youngsters out of doors and free.

Outdoors they scamper to their play
With merry din the livelong day,
And hungrily they jostle in
The favor of the maid to win;
Then, armed with cookies or with cake,
Their way into the yard they make,
And every feathered playmate comes
To gather up his share of crumbs.
The finest garden that I know
Is one where little children grow,
Where cheeks turn brown and eyes are bright,
And all is laughter and delight.

Oh, you may brag of gardens fine,
But let the children race in mine;
And let the roses, white and red,
Make gay the ground whereon they tread.
And who for bloom perfection seeks,
Should mark the color on their cheeks;
No music that the robin spouts
Is equal to their merry shouts;
There is no foliage to compare
With youngsters' sun-kissed, tousled hair:
Spring's greatest joy beyond a doubt
Is when it brings the children out.

REAL SINGING

You can talk about your music, and your
    operatic airs,
And your phonographic record that Caruso's
    tenor bears;
But there isn't any music that such wondrous
    joy can bring
Like the concert when the kiddies and their
    mother start to sing.

When the supper time is over, then the mother
    starts to play
Some simple little ditty, and our concert's under
    way.
And I'm happier and richer than a millionaire
    or king
When I listen to the kiddies and their mother
    as they sing.

There's a sweetness most appealing in the trill-
    ing of their notes:
It is innocence that's pouring from their little
    baby throats;
And I gaze at them enraptured, for my joy's
    a real thing
Every evening when the kiddies and their mother
    start to sing.

THE BUMPS AND BRUISES DOCTOR

I'm the bumps and bruises doctor;
   I'm the expert that they seek
When their rough and tumble playing
   Leaves a scar on leg or cheek.
I'm the rapid, certain curer
   For the wounds of every fall;
I'm the pain eradicator;
   I can always heal them all.

Bumps on little people's foreheads
   I can quickly smooth away;
I take splinters out of fingers
   Without very much delay.
Little sorrows I can banish
   With the magic of my touch;
I can fix a bruise that's dreadful
   So it isn't hurting much.

I'm the bumps and bruises doctor,
   And I answer every call,
And my fee is very simple,
   Just a kiss, and that is all.
And I'm sitting here and wishing
   In the years that are to be,
When they face life's real troubles
   That they'll bring them all to me.

Pa's not so very big or brave; he can't lift
    weights like Uncle Jim;
His hands are soft like little girls'; most anyone
    could wallop him.
Ma weighs a whole lot more than Pa. When
    they go swimming, she could stay
Out in the river all day long, but Pa gets frozen
    right away.
But when the thunder starts to roll, an' lightnin'
    spits, Ma says, " Oh, dear,
I'm sure we'll all of us be killed. I only wish
    your Pa was here."

Pa's cheeks are thin an' kinder pale; he couldn't
    rough it worth a cent.
He couldn't stand the hike we had the day the
    Boy Scouts camping went.
He has to hire a man to dig the garden, coz his
    back gets lame,
An' he'd be crippled for a week, if he should
    play a baseball game.
But when a thunder storm comes up, Ma sits an'
    shivers in the gloam
An' every time the thunder rolls, she says: " I
    wish your Pa was home."

I don't know just what Pa could do if he were
      home, he seems so frail,
But every time the skies grow black I notice Ma
      gets rather pale.
An' when she's called us children in, an' locked
      the windows an' the doors,
She jumps at every lightnin' flash an' trembles
      when the thunder roars.
An' when the baby starts to cry, she wrings her
      hands an' says: "Oh, dear!
It's terrible! It's terrible! I only wish your
      Pa was here."

PEACE

A man must earn his hour of peace,
  Must pay for it with hours of strife and care,
Must win by toil the evening's sweet release,
  The rest that may be portioned for his share;
The idler never knows it, never can.
  Peace is the glory ever of a man.

A man must win contentment for his soul,
  Must battle for it bravely day by day;
The peace he seeks is not a near-by goal;
  To claim it he must tread a rugged way.
The shirker never knows a tranquil breast;
  Peace but rewards the man who does his best.

NO PLACE TO GO

The happiest nights
  I ever know
Are those when I've
  No place to go,
And the missus says
  When the day is through:
" To-night we haven't
  A thing to do."

Oh, the joy of it,
  And the peace untold
Of sitting 'round
  In my slippers old,
With my pipe and book
  In my easy chair,
Knowing I needn't
  Go anywhere.

Needn't hurry
  My evening meal
Nor force the smiles
  That I do not feel,
But can grab a book
  From a near-by shelf,
And drop all sham
  And be myself.

Oh, the charm of it
   And the comfort rare;
Nothing on earth
   With it can compare;
And I'm sorry for him
   Who doesn't know
The joy of having
   No place to go.

DEFEAT

No one is beat till he quits,
   No one is through till he stops,
No matter how hard Failure hits,
   No matter how often he drops,
A fellow's not down till he lies
In the dust and refuses to rise.

Fate can slam him and bang him around,
   And batter his frame till he's sore,
But she never can say that he's downed
   While he bobs up serenely for more.
A fellow's not dead till he dies,
Nor beat till no longer he tries.

A PATRIOTIC WISH

I'd like to be the sort of man the flag could
  boast about;
I'd like to be the sort of man it cannot live
  without;
I'd like to be the type of man
That really is American:
The head-erect and shoulders-square,
Clean-minded fellow, just and fair,
That all men picture when they see
The glorious banner of the free.

I'd like to be the sort of man the flag now
  typifies,
The kind of man we really want the flag to
  symbolize;
The loyal brother to a trust,
The big, unselfish soul and just,
The friend of every man oppressed,
The strong support of all that's best,
The sturdy chap the banner's meant,
Where'er it flies, to represent.

I'd like to be the sort of man the flag's supposed
  to mean,
The man that all in fancy see wherever it is
  seen,
The chap that's ready for a fight
Whenever there's a wrong to right,

The friend in every time of need,
The doer of the daring deed,
The clean and generous handed man
That is a real American.

THE PRICE OF JOY

You don't begrudge the labor when the roses
    start to bloom;
You don't recall the dreary days that won you
    their perfume;
You don't recall a single care
You spent upon the garden there;
And all the toil
Of tilling soil
Is quite forgot the day the first
Pink rosebuds into beauty burst.

You don't begrudge the trials grim when joy
    has come to you;
You don't recall the dreary days when all your
    skies are blue;
And though you've trod a weary mile
The ache of it was all worth while;
And all the stings
And bitter flings
Are wiped away upon the day
Success comes dancing down the way.

THE THINGS THAT MAKE A SOLDIER GREAT

The things that make a soldier great and send
    him out to die,
To face the flaming cannon's mouth nor ever
    question why,
Are lilacs by a little porch, the row of tulips
    red,
The peonies and pansies, too, the old petunia bed,
The grass plot where his children play, the roses
    on the wall:
'Tis these that make a soldier great. He's fight-
    ing for them all.

'Tis not the pomp and pride of kings that make
    a soldier brave;
'Tis not allegiance to the flag that over him may
    wave;
For soldiers never fight so well on land or on
    the foam
As when behind the cause they see the little
    place called home.
Endanger but that humble street whereon his
    children run,
You make a soldier of the man who never bore
    a gun.

What is it through the battle smoke the valiant
    soldier sees?
The little garden far away, the budding apple
    trees,
The little patch of ground back there, the chil-
    dren at their play,
Perhaps a tiny mound behind the simple church
    of gray.
The golden thread of courage isn't linked to
    castle dome
But to the spot, where'er it be — the humble spot
    called home.

And now the lilacs bud again and all is lovely
    there
And homesick soldiers far away know spring
    is in the air;
The tulips come to bloom again, the grass
    once more is green,
And every man can see the spot where all his
    joys have been.
He sees his children smile at him, he hears the
    bugle call,
And only death can stop him now — he's fight-
    ing for them all.

THE JOY OF A DOG

Ma says no, it's too much care
An' it will scatter germs an' hair,
An' it's a nuisance through and through.
An' barks when you don't want it to;
An' carries dirt from off the street,
An' tracks the carpets with its feet.
But it's a sign he's growin' up
When he is longin' for a pup.

Most every night he comes to me
An' climbs a-straddle of my knee
An' starts to fondle me an' pet,
Then asks me if I've found one yet.
An' ma says: " Now don't tell him yes;
You know they make an awful mess,"
An' starts their faults to catalogue.
But every boy should have a dog.

An' some night when he comes to me,
Deep in my pocket there will be
The pup he's hungry to possess
Or else I sadly miss my guess.
For I remember all the joy
A dog meant to a little boy
Who loved it in the long ago,
The joy that's now his right to know.

HOMESICK

It's tough when you are homesick in a strange
    and distant place;
It's anguish when you're hungry for an old-
    familiar face.
And yearning for the good folks and the joys
    you used to know,
When you're miles away from friendship, is a
    bitter sort of woe.
But it's tougher, let me tell you, and a stiffer
    discipline
To see them through the window, and to know
    you can't go in.

Oh, I never knew the meaning of that red sign
    on the door,
Never really understood it, never thought of it
    before;
But I'll never see another since they've tacked
    one up on mine
But I'll think about the father that is barred
    from all that's fine.
And I'll think about the mother who is prisoner
    in there
So her little son or daughter shall not miss a
    mother's care.
And I'll share a fellow feeling with the saddest
    of my kin,
The dad beside the gateway of the home he
    can't go in.

Oh, we laugh and joke together and the mother
    tries to be
Brave and sunny in her prison, and she thinks
    she's fooling me;
And I do my bravest smiling and I feign a
    merry air
In the hope she won't discover that I'm bur-
    dened down with care.
But it's only empty laughter, and there's nothing
    in the grin
When you're talking through the window of the
    home you can't go in.

THE PERFECT DINNER TABLE

A table cloth that's slightly soiled
Where greasy little hands have toiled;
The napkins kept in silver rings,
And only ordinary things
From which to eat, a simple fare,
And just the wife and kiddies there,
And while I serve, the clatter glad
Of little girl and little lad
Who have so very much to say
About the happenings of the day.

Four big round eyes that dance with glee,
Forever flashing joys at me,
Two little tongues that race and run
To tell of troubles and of fun;

The mother with a patient smile
Who knows that she must wait awhile
Before she'll get a chance to say
What she's discovered through the day.
She steps aside for girl and lad
Who have so much to tell their dad.

Our manners may not be the best;
Perhaps our elbows often rest
Upon the table, and at times
That very worst of dinner crimes,
That very shameful act and rude
Of speaking ere you've downed your food,
Too frequently, I fear, is done,
So fast the little voices run.
Yet why should table manners stay
Those tongues that have so much to say?

At many a table I have been
Where wealth and luxury were seen,
And I have dined in halls of pride
Where all the guests were dignified;
But when it comes to pleasure rare
The perfect dinner table's where
No stranger's face is ever known:
The dinner hour we spend alone,
When little girl and little lad
Run riot telling things to dad,

TO-MORROW

He was going to be all that a mortal should be
> To-morrow.
No one should be kinder or braver than he
> To-morrow.
A friend who was troubled and weary he knew,
Who'd be glad of a lift and who needed it, too;
On him he would call and see what he could do
> To-morrow.

Each morning he stacked up the letters he'd
> write
> To-morrow.
And thought of the folks he would fill with
> delight
> To-morrow.
It was too bad, indeed, he was busy to-day,
And hadn't a minute to stop on his way;
More time he would have to give others, he'd
> say,
> To-morrow.

The greatest of workers this man would have
> been
> To-morrow.
The world would have known him, had he ever
> seen
> To-morrow.

But the fact is he died and he faded from view,
And all that he left here when living was
  through
Was a mountain of things he intended to do
   To-morrow.

A PRAYER

God grant me kindly thought
 And patience through the day,
And in the things I've wrought
 Let no man living say
That hate's grim mark has stained
What little joy I've gained.

God keep my nature sweet,
 Teach me to bear a blow,
Disaster and defeat,
 And no resentment show.
If failure must be mine
Sustain this soul of mine.

God grant me strength to face
 Undaunted day or night;
To stoop to no disgrace
 To win my little fight;
Let me be, when it is o'er,
As manly as before.

TO THE LADY IN THE ELECTRIC

Lady in the show case carriage,
  Do not think that I'm a bear;
Not for worlds would I disparage
  One so gracious and so fair;
Do not think that I am blind to
  One who has a smile seraphic;
You I'd never be unkind to,
  But you are impeding traffic.

If I had some way of knowing
  What you are about to do,
Just exactly where you're going,
  If I could depend on you,
I could keep my engine churning,
  Travel on and never mind you.
Lady, when you think of turning,
  Why not signal us behind you?

Lady, free from care and worry,
  Riding in your plate-glass car,
Some of us are in a hurry;
  Some of us must travel far.
I, myself, am eager, very,
  To be journeying on my way;
Lady, is it necessary
  To monopolize the highway?

Lady, at the handle, steering,
    Why not keep a course that's straight?
Know you not that wildly veering
    As you do, is tempting fate?
Do not think my horn I'm blowing
    Just on purpose to harass you,
It is just a signal showing
    That I'd safely like to pass you.

Lady, there are times a duty
    Must be done, however saddening;
It is hard to tell a beauty
    That she's very often maddening.
And I would not now be saying
    Harsh and cruel words to fuss you,
But when traffic you're delaying
    You are forcing men to cuss you.

THE MAN WHO COULDN'T SAVE

He spent what he made, or he gave it away,
Tried to save money, and would for a day,
Started a bank-account time an' again,
Got a hundred or so for a nest egg, an' then
Some fellow that needed it more than he did,
Who was down on his luck, with a sick wife
or kid,
Came along an' he wasted no time till he went
An' drew out the coin that for saving was
meant.

They say he died poor, and I guess that is so:
To pile up a fortune he hadn't a show;
He worked all the time and good money he made,
Was known as an excellent man at his trade,
But he saw too much, heard too much, felt too
much here
To save anything by the end of the year,
An' the shabbiest wreck the Lord ever let live
Could get money from him if he had it to give.

I've seen him slip dimes to the bums on the street
Who told him they hungered for something to
eat,
An' though I remarked they were going for
drink
He'd say: "Mebbe so. But I'd just hate to
think

That fellow was hungry an' I'd passed him by;
I'd rather be fooled twenty times by a lie
Than wonder if one of 'em I wouldn't feed
Had told me the truth an' was really in need."

Never stinted his family out of a thing:
They had everything that his money could bring;
Said he'd rather be broke and just know they
　　　were glad,
Than rich, with them pining an' wishing they had
Some of the pleasures his money would buy;
Said he never could look a bank book in the eye
If he knew it had grown on the pleasures and
　　　joys
That he'd robbed from his wife and his girls
　　　and his boys.

Queer sort of notion he had, I confess,
Yet many a rich man on earth is mourned less.
All who had known him came back to his side
To honor his name on the day that he died.
Didn't leave much in the bank, it is true,
But did leave a fortune in people who knew
The big heart of him, an' I'm willing to swear
That to-day he is one of the richest up there.

ANSWERING HIM

" When shall I be a man? " he said,
As I was putting him to bed.
" How many years will have to be
Before Time makes a man of me?
And will I be a man when I
Am grown up big? " I heaved a sigh,
Because it called for careful thought
To give the answer that he sought.

And so I sat him on my knee,
And said to him: " A man you'll be
When you have learned that honor brings
More joy than all the crowns of kings;
That it is better to be true
To all who know and trust in you
Than all the gold of earth to gain
If winning it shall leave a stain.

" When you can fight for victory sweet,
Yet bravely swallow down defeat,
And cling to hope and keep the right,
Nor use deceit instead of might;
When you are kind and brave and clean,
And fair to all and never mean;
When there is good in all you plan,
That day, my boy, you'll be a man.

" Some of us learn this truth too late;
That years alone can't make us great;
That many who are three-score, ten
Have fallen short of being men,
Because in selfishness they fought
And toiled without refining thought;
And whether wrong or whether right
They lived but for their own delight.

" When you have learned that you must hold
Your honor dearer far than gold;
That no ill-gotten wealth or fame
Can pay you for your tarnished name;
And when in all you say or do
Of others you're considerate, too,
Content to do the best you can
By such a creed, you'll be a man."

FATHER AND SON

Be more than his dad,
Be a chum to the lad;
Be a part of his life
Every hour of the day;
Find time to talk with him,
Take time to walk with him,
Share in his studies
And share in his play;
Take him to places,
To ball games and races,
Teach him the things
That you want him to know;
Don't live apart from him,
Don't keep your heart from him,
Be his best comrade,
He's needing you so!

Never neglect him,
Though young, still respect him,
Hear his opinions
With patience and pride;
Show him his error,
But be not a terror,
Grim-visaged and fearful,
When he's at your side.

Know what his thoughts are,
Know what his sports are,
Know all his playmates,
It's easy to learn to;
Be such a father
That when troubles gather
You'll be the first one
For counsel, he'll turn to.

You can inspire him
With courage, and fire him
Hot with ambition
For deeds that are good;
He'll not betray you
Nor illy repay you,
If you have taught him
The things that you should.
Father and son
Must in all things be one —
Partners in trouble
And comrades in joy.
More than a dad
Was the best pal you had;
Be such a chum
As you knew, to your boy.

THE JUNE COUPLE

She is fair to see and sweet,
Dainty from her head to feet,
Modest, as her blushing shows,
Happy, as her smiles disclose,
And the young man at her side
Nervously attempts to hide
Underneath a visage grim
That the fuss is bothering him.

Pause a moment, happy pair!
This is not the station where
Romance ends, and wooing stops
And the charm from courtship drops;
This is but the outward gate
Where the souls of mortals mate,
But the border of the land
You must travel hand in hand.

You who come to marriage, bring
All your tenderness, and cling
Steadfastly to all the ways
That have marked your wooing days.
You are only starting out
On life's roadways, hedged about
Thick with roses and with tares,
Sweet delights and bitter cares.

Heretofore you've only played
At love's game, young man and maid;
Only known it at its best;
Now you'll have to face its test.
You must prove your love worth while,
Something time cannot defile,
Something neither care nor pain
Can destroy or mar or stain.

You are now about to show
Whether love is real or no;
Yonder down the lane of life
You will find, as man and wife,
Sorrows, disappointments, doubt,
Hope will almost flicker out;
But if rightly you are wed
Love will linger where you tread.

There are joys that you will share,
Joys to balance every care;
Arm in arm remain, and you
Will not fear the storms that brew,
If when you are sorest tried
You face your trials, side by side.
Now your wooing days are done,
And your loving years begun.

AT THE DOOR

He wiped his shoes before his door,
But ere he entered he did more:
'Twas not enough to cleanse his feet
Of dirt they'd gathered in the street;
He stood and dusted off his mind
And left all trace of care behind.
"In here I will not take," said he,
"The stains the day has brought to me.

"Beyond this door shall never go
The burdens that are mine to know;
The day is done, and here I leave
The petty things that vex and grieve;
What clings to me of hate and sin
To them I will not carry in;
Only the good shall go with me
For their devoted eyes to see.

"I will not burden them with cares,
Nor track the home with grim affairs;
I will not at my table sit
With soul unclean, and mind unfit;
Beyond this door I will not take
The outward signs of inward ache;
I will not take a dreary mind
Into this house for them to find."

He wiped his shoes before his door,
But paused to do a little more.

He dusted off the stains of strife,
The mud that's incident to life,
The blemishes of careless thought,
The traces of the fight he'd fought,
The selfish humors and the mean,
And when he entered he was clean.

DUTY

To do your little bit of toil,
 To play life's game with head erect;
To stoop to nothing that would soil
 Your honor or your self-respect;
To win what gold and fame you can,
But first of all to be a man.

To know the bitter and the sweet,
 The sunshine and the days of rain;
To meet both victory and defeat,
 Nor boast too loudly nor complain;
To face whatever fates befall
And be a man throughout it all.

To seek success in honest strife,
 But not to value it so much
That, winning it, you go through life
 Stained by dishonor's scarlet touch.
What goal or dream you choose, pursue,
But be a man whate'er you do!

A BEAR STORY

There was a bear — his name was Jim,
An' children weren't askeered of him,
An' he lived in a cave, where he
Was confortubbul as could be,
An' in that cave, so my Pa said,
Jim always kept a stock of bread
An' honey, so that he could treat
The boys an' girls along his street.

An' all that Jim could say was " Woof! "
An' give a grunt that went like " Soof! "
An' Pa says when his grunt went off
It sounded jus' like Grandpa's cough,
Or like our Jerry when he's mad
An' growls at peddler men that's bad.
While grown-ups were afraid of Jim,
Kids could do anything with him.

One day a little boy like me
That had a sister Marjorie,
Was walking through the woods, an' they
Heard something " woofing " down that way,
An' they was scared an' stood stock still
An' wished they had a gun to kill
Whatever 'twas, but little boys
Don't have no guns that make a noise.

An' soon the " woofing " closer grew,
An' then a bear came into view,
The biggest bear you ever saw —
Ma's muff was smaller than his paw.
He saw the children an' he said:
" I ain't a-goin' to kill you dead;
You needn't turn away an' run;
I'm only scarin' you for fun."

An' then he stood up just like those
Big bears in circuses an' shows,
An' danced a jig, an' rolled about
An' said " Woof! Woof!" which meant " Look
        out!"
An' turned a somersault as slick
As any boy can do the trick.
Those children had been told of Jim
An' they decided it was him.

They stroked his nose when they got brave,
An' followed him into his cave,
An' Jim asked them if they liked honey,
They said they did.   Said Jim: " That's funny.
I've asked a thousand boys or so
That question, an' not one's said no."
What happened then I cannot say
'Cause next I knew 'twas light as day.

AUTUMN AT THE ORCHARD

The sumac's flaming scarlet on the edges o' the
    lake,
An' the pear trees are invitin' everyone t' come
    an' shake.
Now the gorgeous tints of autumn are appearin'
    everywhere
Till it seems that you can almost see the Master
    Painter there.
There's a solemn sort o' stillness that's pervadin'
    every thing,
Save the farewell songs to summer that the
    feathered tenors sing,
An' you quite forget the city where disgruntled
    folks are kickin'
Off yonder with the Pelletiers, when spies are
    ripe fer pickin'.

The Holsteins are a-posin' in a clearin' near a
    wood,
Very dignified an' stately, just as though they
    understood
That they're lending to life's pictures just the
    touch the Master needs,
An' they're preachin' more refinement than a lot
    o' printed creeds.
The orchard's fairly groanin' with the gifts o'
    God to man,
Just as though they meant to shame us who
    have doubted once His plan.

Oh, there's somethin' most inspirin' to a soul in
    need o' prickin'
Off yonder with the Pelletiers when spies are
    ripe fer pickin'.

The frisky little Shetlands now are growin'
    shaggy coats
An' acquirin' silken mufflers of their own to
    guard their throats;
An' a Russian wolf-hound puppy left its mother
    yesterday,
An' a tinge o' sorrow touched us as we saw it
    go away.
For the sight was full o' meanin', an' we knew,
    when it had gone,
'Twas a symbol of the partin's that the years are
    bringin' on.
Oh, a feller must be better — to his faith he can't
    help stickin'
Off yonder with the Pelletiers when spies are ripe
    fer pickin'.

The year is almost over, now at dusk the valleys
    glow
With the misty mantle chillin', that is hangin'
    very low.
An' each mornin' sees the maples just a little
    redder turned
Than they were the night we left 'em, an' the
    elms are browner burned.

An' a feller can't help feelin', an' I don't care
    who it is,
That the mind that works such wonders has a
    greater power than his.
Oh, I know that I'll remember till life's last few
    sparks are flickin'
The lessons out at Pelletiers when spies were ripe
    for pickin'.

WHEN PA COMES HOME

When Pa comes home, I'm at the door,
An' then he grabs me off the floor
An' throws me up an' catches me
When I come down, an' then, says he:
" Well, how'd you get along to-day?
An' were you good, an' did you play,
An' keep right out of mamma's way?
An' how'd you get that awful bump
Above your eye? My, what a lump!
An' who spilled jelly on your shirt?
An' where'd you ever find the dirt
That's on your hands? And my! Oh, my!
I guess those eyes have had a cry,
They look so red. What was it, pray?
What has been happening here to-day?"

An' then he drops his coat an' hat
Upon a chair, an' says: " What's that?

Who knocked that engine on its back
An' stepped upon that piece of track?"
An' then he takes me on his knee
An' says: "What's this that now I see?
Whatever can the matter be?
Who strewed those toys upon the floor,
An' left those things behind the door?
Who upset all those parlor chairs
An' threw those blocks upon the stairs?
I guess a cyclone called to-day
While I was workin' far away.
Who was it worried mamma so?
It can't be anyone I know."

An' then I laugh an' say: "It's me!
Me did most ever'thing you see.
Me got this bump the time me tripped.
An' here is where the jelly slipped
Right off my bread upon my shirt,
An' when me tumbled down it hurt.
That's how me got all over dirt.
Me threw those building blocks downstairs,
An' me upset the parlor chairs,
Coz when you're playin' train you've got
To move things 'round an awful lot."
An' then my Pa he kisses me
An' bounces me upon his knee
An' says: "Well, well, my little lad,
What glorious fun you must have had!"

MOTHER'S DAY

Gentle hands that never weary toiling in love's
    vineyard sweet,
Eyes that seem forever cheery when our eyes
    they chance to meet,
Tender, patient, brave, devoted, this is always
    mother's way.
Could her worth in gold be quoted as you think
    of her to-day?

There shall never be another quite so tender,
    quite so kind
As the patient little mother; nowhere on this
    earth you'll find
Her affection duplicated; none so proud if you
    are fine.
Could her worth be overstated? Not by any
    words of mine.

Death stood near the hour she bore us, agony
    was hers to know,
Yet she bravely faced it for us, smiling in her
    time of woe;
Down the years how oft we've tried her, often
    selfish, heedless, blind,
Yet with love alone to guide her she was never
    once unkind.

Vain are all our tributes to her if in words
    alone they dwell.
We must live the praises due her; there's no
    other way to tell
Gentle mother that we love her. Would you say,
    as you recall
All the patient service of her, you've been
    worthy of it all?

DIVISION

You cannot gather every rose,
    Nor every pleasure claim,
Nor bask in every breeze that blows,
    Nor play in every game.

No millionaire could ever own
    The world's supply of pearls,
And no man here has ever known
    All of the pretty girls.

So take what joy may come your way,
    And envy not your brothers;
Enjoy your share of fun each day,
    And leave the rest for others.

A MAN

A man doesn't whine at his losses.
  A man doesn't whimper and fret,
Or rail at the weight of his crosses
  And ask life to rear him a pet.
A man doesn't grudgingly labor
  Or look upon toil as a blight;
A man doesn't sneer at his neighbor
  Or sneak from a cause that is right.

A man doesn't sulk when another
  Succeeds where his efforts have failed;
Doesn't keep all his praise for the brother
  Whose glory is publicly hailed;
And pass by the weak and the humble
  As though they were not of his clay;
A man doesn't ceaselessly grumble
  When things are not going his way.

A man looks on woman as tender
  And gentle, and stands at her side
At all times to guard and defend her,
  And never to scorn or deride.
A man looks on life as a mission.
  To serve, just so far as he can;
A man holds his noblest ambition
  On earth is to live as a man.

A VOW

I might not ever scale the mountain heights
    Where all the great men stand in glory now;
I may not ever gain the world's delights
    Or win a wreath of laurel for my brow;
I may not gain the victories that men
    Are fighting for, nor do a thing to boast of;
I may not get a fortune here, but then,
    The little that I have I'll make the most of.

I'll make my little home a palace fine,
    My little patch of green a garden fair,
And I shall know each humble plant and vine
    As rich men know their orchid blossoms rare.
My little home may not be much to see;
    Its chimneys may not tower far above;
But it will be a mansion great to me,
    For in its walls I'll keep a hoard of love.

I will not pass my modest pleasures by
    To grasp at shadows of more splendid things,
Disdaining what of joyousness is nigh
    Because I am denied the joy of kings.
But I will laugh and sing my way along,
    I'll make the most of what is mine to-day,
And if I never rise above the throng,
    I shall have lived a full life anyway.

TREASURES

Some folks I know, when friends drop in
To visit for awhile and chin,
Just lead them round the rooms and halls
And show them pictures on their walls,
And point to rugs and tapestries
The works of men across the seas:
Their loving cups they show with pride,
To eyes that soon are stretching wide
With wonder at the treasures rare
That have been bought and gathered there.

But when folks come to call on me,
I've no such things for them to see.
No picture on my walls is great;
I have no ancient family plate;
No tapestry of rare design
Or costly woven rugs are mine;
I have no loving cup to show,
Or strange and valued curio;
But if my treasures they would see,
I bid them softly follow me.

And then I lead them up the stairs
Through trains of cars and Teddy bears,
And to a little room we creep
Where both my youngsters lie asleep,
Close locked in one another's arms.
I let them gaze upon their charms,

I let them see the legs of brown
Curled up beneath a sleeping gown,
And whisper in my happiness:
"Behold the treasures I possess."

CHALLENGE

Life is a challenge to the bold,
   It flings its gauntlet down
And bids us, if we seek for gold
   And glory and renown,
To come and *take* them from its store,
It will not meekly hand them o'er.

Life is a challenge all must meet,
   And nobly must we dare;
Its gold is tawdry when we cheat,
   Its fame a bitter snare
If it be stolen from life's clutch;
Men must be true to prosper much.

Life is a challenge and its laws
   Are rigid ones and stern;
The splendid joy of real applause
   Each man must nobly earn.
It makes us win its jewels rare,
But gives us paste, if we're unfair.

A TOAST TO HAPPINESS

To happiness I raise my glass,
 The goal of every human,
The hope of every clan and class
 And every man and woman.
The daydreams of the urchin there,
The sweet theme of the maiden's prayer,
 The strong man's one ambition,
The sacred prize of mothers sweet,
The tramp of soldiers on the street
 Have all the selfsame mission.
Life here is nothing more nor less
Than just a quest for happiness.

Some seek it on the mountain top,
 And some within a mine;
The widow in her notion shop
 Expects its sun to shine.
The tramp that seeks new roads to fare,
Is one with king and millionaire
 In this that each is groping
On different roads, in different ways,
To come to glad, contented days,
 And shares the common hoping.
The sound of martial fife and drum
Is born of happiness to come.

Yet happiness is always here
  Had we the eyes to see it;
No breast but holds a fund of cheer
  Had man the will to free it.
'Tis there upon the mountain top,
Or in the widow's notion shop,
  'Tis found in homes of sorrow;
'Tis woven in the memories
Of happier, brighter days than these,
  The gift, not of to-morrow
But of to-day, and in our tears
Some touch of happiness appears.

'Tis not a joy that's born of wealth:
  The poor man may possess it.
'Tis not alone the prize of health:
  No sickness can repress it.
'Tis not the end of mortal strife,
The sunset of the day of life,
  Or but the old should find it;
It is the bond twixt God and man,
The touch divine in all we plan,
  And has the soul behind it.
And so this toast to happiness,
The seed of which we all possess.

GUESSING TIME

It's guessing time at our house; every evening
    after tea
We start guessing what old Santa's going to
    leave us on our tree.
Everyone of us holds secrets that the others try
    to steal,
And that eyes and lips are plainly having trouble
    to conceal.
And a little lip that quivered just a bit the other
    night
Was a sad and startling warning that I mustn't
    guess it right.

" Guess what you will get for Christmas! " is the
    cry that starts the fun.
And I answer: " Give the letter with which the
    name's begun."
Oh, the eyes that dance around me and the joy-
    ous faces there
Keep me nightly guessing wildly: " Is it some-
    thing I can wear? "
I implore them all to tell me in a frantic sort
    of way
And pretend that I am puzzled, just to keep them
    feeling gay.

Oh, the wise and knowing glances that across the
  table fly
And the winks exchanged with mother, that they
  think I never spy;
Oh, the whispered confidences that are poured
  into her ear,
And the laughter gay that follows when I try
  my best to hear!
Oh, the shouts of glad derision when I bet that
  it's a cane,
And the merry answering chorus: "No, it's
  not. Just guess again!"

It's guessing time at our house, and the fun is
  running fast,
And I wish somehow this contest of delight
  could always last,
For the love that's in their faces and their laugh-
  ter ringing clear
Is their dad's most precious present when the
  Christmas time is near.
And soon as it is over, when the tree is bare
  and plain,
I shall start in looking forward to the time to
  guess again.

UNDERSTANDING

When I was young and frivolous and never
    stopped to think,
When I was always doing wrong, or just upon
    the brink;
When I was just a lad of seven and eight and
    nine and ten,
It seemed to me that every day I got in trouble
    then,
And strangers used to shake their heads and say
    I was no good,
But father always stuck to me — it seems he
    understood.

I used to have to go to him 'most every night
    and say
The dreadful things that I had done to worry
    folks that day.
I know I didn't mean to be a turmoil round the
    place,
And with the womenfolks about forever in dis-
    grace;
To do the way they said I should, I tried the
    best I could,
But though they scolded me a lot — my father
    understood.

He never seemed to think it queer that I should
    risk my bones,
Or fight with other boys at times, or pelt a cat
    with stones;
An' when I'd break a window pane, it used to
    make him sad,
But though the neighbors said I was, he never
    thought me bad;
He never whipped me, as they used to say to me
    he should;
That boys can't always do what's right — it
    seemed he understood.

Now there's that little chap of mine, just full of
    life and fun,
Comes up to me with solemn face to tell the
    bad he's done.
It's natural for any boy to be a roguish elf,
He hasn't time to stop and think and figure for
    himself,
And though the womenfolks insist that I should
    take a hand,
They've never been a boy themselves, and they
    don't understand.

Some day I've got to go up there, and make a
    sad report

And tell the Father of us all where I have fallen
    short;
And there will be a lot of wrong I never meant
    to do,
A lot of smudges on my sheet that He will have
    to view.
And little chance for heavenly bliss, up there,
    will I command,
Unless the Father smiles and says: "My boy,
    I understand."

PEOPLE LIKED HIM

People liked him, not because
    He was rich or known to fame;
He had never won applause
    As a star in any game.
His was not a brilliant style,
    His was not a forceful way,
But he had a gentle smile
    And a kindly word to say.

Never arrogant or proud,
    On he went with manner mild;
Never quarrelsome or loud,
    Just as simple as a child;
Honest, patient, brave and true:
    Thus he lived from day to day,
Doing what he found to do
    In a cheerful sort of way.

Wasn't one to boast of gold
  Or belittle it with sneers,
Didn't change from hot to cold,
  Kept his friends throughout the years,
Sort of man you like to meet
  Any time or any place.
There was always something sweet
  And refreshing in his face.

Sort of man you'd like to be:
  Balanced well and truly square;
Patient in adversity,
  Generous when his skies were fair.
Never lied to friend or foe,
  Never rash in word or deed,
Quick to come and slow to go
  In a neighbor's time of need.

Never rose to wealth or fame,
  Simply lived, and simply died,
But the passing of his name
  Left a sorrow, far and wide.
Not for glory he'd attained,
  Nor for what he had of pelf,
Were the friends that he had gained,
  But for what he was himself.

WHEN FATHER SHOOK THE STOVE

'Twas not so many years ago,
  Say, twenty-two or three,
When zero weather or below
  Held many a thrill for me.
Then in my icy room I slept
  A youngster's sweet repose,
And always on my form I kept
  My flannel underclothes.
Then I was roused by sudden shock
  Though still to sleep I strove,
I knew that it was seven o'clock
  When father shook the stove.

I never heard him quit his bed
  Or his alarm clock ring;
I never heard his gentle tread,
  Or his attempts to sing;
The sun that found my window pane
  On me was wholly lost,
Though many a sunbeam tried in vain
  To penetrate the frost.
To human voice I never stirred,
  But deeper down I dove
Beneath the covers, when I heard
  My father shake the stove.

To-day it all comes back to me
    And I can hear it still;
He seemed to take a special glee
    In shaking with a will.
He flung the noisy dampers back,
    Then rattled steel on steel,
Until the force of his attack
    The building seemed to feel.
Though I'd a youngster's heavy eyes
    All sleep from them he drove;
It seemed to me the dead must rise
    When father shook the stove.

Now radiators thump and pound
    And every room is warm,
And modern men new ways have found
    To shield us from the storm.
The window panes are seldom glossed
    The way they used to be;
The pictures left by old Jack Frost
    Our children never see.
And now that he has gone to rest
    In God's great slumber grove,
I often think those days were best
    When father shook the stove.

HOUSE-HUNTING

Time was when spring returned we went
To find another home to rent;
We wanted fresher, cleaner walls,
And bigger rooms and wider halls,
And open plumbing and the dome
That made the fashionable home.

But now with spring we want to sell,
And seek a finer place to dwell.
Our thoughts have turned from dens and domes;
We want the latest thing in homes;
To life we'll not be reconciled
Until we have a bathroom tiled.

A butler's pantry we desire,
Although no butler do we hire;
Nell's life will be one round of gloom
Without a closet for the broom,
And mine will dreary be and sour
Unless the bathroom has a shower.

For months and months we've sat and dreamed
Of paneled walls and ceilings beamed
And built-in cases for the books,
An attic room to be the cook's.
No house will she consent to view
Unless it has a sun room, too.

There must be wash bowls here and there
To save much climbing of the stair;
A sleeping porch we both demand —
This fad has swept throughout the land —
And, Oh, 'twill give her heart a wrench
Not to possess a few doors, French.

I want to dig and walk around
At least full fifty feet of ground;
She wants the latest style in tubs;
I want more room for trees and shrubs,
And a garage, with light and heat,
That can be entered from the street.

The trouble is the things we seek
Cannot be bought for ten-a-week.
And all the joys for which we sigh
Are just too rich for us to buy.
We have the taste to cut a dash:
The thing we're lacking most is cash.

AN EASY WORLD

It's an easy world to live in if you choose to
    make it so;
You never need to suffer, save the griefs that
    all must know;
If you'll stay upon the level and will do the
    best you can
You will never lack the friendship of a kindly
    fellow man.

Life's an easy road to travel if you'll only walk
    it straight;
There are many here to help you in your little
    bouts with fate;
When the clouds begin to gather and your hopes
    begin to fade,
If you've only toiled in honor you won't have
    to call for aid.

But if you've bartered friendship and the faith
    on which it rests
For a temporary winning; if you've cheated in
    the tests,
If with promises you've broken, you have chilled
    the hearts of men;
It is vain to look for friendship for it will not
    come again.

Oh, the world is full of kindness, thronged with
      men who want to be
Of some service to their neighbors and they'll
      run to you or me
When we're needing their assistance if we've
      lived upon the square,
But they'll spurn us in our trouble if we've
      always been unfair.

It's an easy world to live in; all you really need
      to do
Is the decent thing and proper and then friends
      will flock to you;
But let dishonor trail you and some stormy day
      you'll find
To your heart's supremest sorrow that you've
      made the world unkind.

THE STATES

There is no star within the flag
   That's brighter than its brothers,
And when of Michigan I brag,
   I'm boasting of the others.
Just which is which no man can say —
   One star for every state
Gleams brightly on our flag to-day,
   And every one is great.

The stars that gem the skies at night
   May differ in degree,
And some are pale and some are bright,
   But in our flag we see
A sky of blue wherein the stars
   Are equal in design;
Each has the radiance of Mars
   And all are yours and mine.

The glory that is Michigan's
   Is Colorado's too;
The same sky Minnesota spans,
   The same sun warms it through;
And all are one beneath the flag,
   A common hope is ours;
Our country is the mountain crag,
   The valley and its flowers.

The land we love lies far away
  As well as close at hand;
He has no vision who would say:
  This state's my native land.
Though sweet the charms he knows the best,
  Deep down within his heart
The farthest east, the farthest west
  Of him must be a part.

There is no star within the flag
  That's brighter than its brothers;
So when of Michigan I brag
  I'm boasting of the others.
We share alike one purpose true;
  One common end awaits;
We must in all we dream or do
  Remain *United* States.

THE OBLIGATION OF FRIENDSHIP

You ought to be fine for the sake of the folks
      Who think you are fine.
If others have faith in you doubly you're bound
      To stick to the line.
It's not only on you that dishonor descends:
You can't hurt yourself without hurting your
      friends.

You ought to be true for the sake of the folks
      Who believe you are true.
You never should stoop to a deed that your
      friends
      Think you wouldn't do.
If you're false to yourself, be the blemish but
      small,
You have injured your friends; you've been false
      to them all.

For friendship, my boy, is a bond between men
      That is founded on truth:
It believes in the best of the ones that it loves,
      Whether old man or youth;
And the stern rule it lays down for me and for
      you
Is to be what our friends think we are, through
      and through.

UNDER THE SKIN OF MEN

Did you ever sit down and talk with men
    In a serious sort of a way,
On their views of life and ponder then
    On all that they have to say?
If not, you should in some quiet hour;
    It's a glorious thing to do:
For you'll find that back of the pomp and power
    Most men have a goal in view.

They'll tell you then that their aim is not
    The clink of the yellow gold;
That not in the worldly things they've got
    Would they have their stories told.
They'll say the joys that they treasure most
    Are their good friends, tried and true,
And an honest name for their own to boast
    And peace when the day is through.

I've talked with men and I think I know
    What's under the toughened skin.
I've seen their eyes grow bright and glow
    With the fire that burns within.
And back of the gold and back of the fame
    And back of the selfish strife,
In most men's breasts you'll find the flame
    Of the nobler things of life.

THE FINER THOUGHT

How fine it is at night to say:
" I have not wronged a soul to-day.
I have not by a word or deed,
In any breast sowed anger's seed,
Or caused a fellow being pain;
Nor is there on my crest a stain
That shame has left.   In honor's way,
With head erect, I've lived this day."

When night slips down and day departs
And rest returns to weary hearts,
How fine it is to close the book
Of records for the day, and look
Once more along the traveled mile
And find that all has been worth while;
To say: " In honor I have toiled;
My plume is spotless and unsoiled."

Yet cold and stern a man may be
Retaining his integrity;
And he may pass from day to day
A spirit dead, in living clay,
Observing strictly morals, laws,
Yet serving but a selfish cause;
So it is not enough to say:
" I have not stooped to shame to-day! "

It is a finer, nobler thought
When day is done and night has brought
The contemplative hours and sweet,
And rest to weary hearts and feet,
If man can stand in truth and say:
" I have been useful here to-day.
Back there is one I chanced to see
With hope newborn because of me.

" This day in honor I have toiled;
My shining crest is still unsoiled;
But on the mile I leave behind
Is one who says that I was kind;
And someone hums a cheerful song
Because I chanced to come along."
Sweet rest at night that man shall own
Who has not lived his day alone.

STUCK

I'm up against it day by day,
  My ignorance is distressing;
The things I don't know on the way
  I'm busily confessing.
Time was I used to think I knew
  Some useful bits of knowledge
And could be sure of one or two
  Real facts I'd gleaned in college.
But I'm unfitted for the task
Of answering things my boy can ask.

Now, who can answer queries queer
  That four-year-olds can think up?
And tell in simple phrase and clear
  Why fishes do not drink up
The water in the streams and lakes,
  Or where the wind is going,
And tell exactly how God makes
  The roses that are growing?
I'm sure I cannot satisfy
Each little when, and how, and why.

Had I the wisdom of a sage
  Possessed of all the learning
That can be gleaned from printed page
  From bookworm's closest turning,
That eager knowledge-seeking lad
  That questions me so gayly

Could still go round and boast he had
　　With queries floored me daily.
He'll stick, I'll bet, in less than five
Brief minutes any man alive.

ETERNAL FRIENDSHIP

Who once has had a friend has found
　　The link 'twixt mortal and divine;
Though now he sleeps in hallowed ground,
　　He lives in memory's sacred shrine;
And there he freely moves about,
　　A spirit that has quit the clay,
And in the times of stress and doubt
　　Sustains his friend throughout the day.

No friend we love can ever die;
　　The outward form but disappears;
I know that all my friends are nigh
　　Whenever I am moved to tears.
And when my strength and hope are gone,
　　The friends, no more, that once I knew,
Return to cheer and urge me on
　　Just as they always used to do.

They whisper to me in the dark
　　Kind words of counsel and of cheer;
When hope has flickered to a spark
　　I feel their gentle spirits near.

And Oh! because of them I strive
  With all the strength that I can call
To keep their friendship still alive
  And to be worthy of them all.

Death does not end our friendships true;
  We all are debtors to the dead;
There, wait on everything we do
  The splendid souls who've gone ahead.
To them I hold that we are bound
  By double pledges to be fine.
Who once has had a friend has found
  The link 'twixt mortal and divine.

FAITH

I believe in the world and its bigness and
    splendor:
That most of the hearts beating round us are
    tender;
That days are but footsteps and years are but
    miles
That lead us to beauty and singing and smiles:
That roses that blossom and toilers that plod
Are filled with the glorious spirit of God.

I believe in the purpose of everything living:
That taking is but the forerunner of giving;

That strangers are friends that we some day
      may meet;
And not all the bitter can equal the sweet;
That creeds are but colors, and no man has
      said
That God loves the yellow rose more than the
      red.

I believe in the path that to-day I am treading,
That I shall come safe through the dangers I'm
      dreading;
That even the scoffer shall turn from his ways
And some day be won back to trust and to
      praise;
That the leaf on the tree and the thing we call
      Man
Are sharing alike in His infinite plan.

I believe that all things that are living and
      breathing
Some richness of beauty to earth are bequeath-
      ing;
That all that goes out of this world leaves
      behind
Some duty accomplished for mortals to find;
That the humblest of creatures our praise is
      deserving,
For it, with the wisest, the Master is serving.

I

Nobody hates me more than I;
   No enemy have I to-day
That I so bravely must defy;
   There are no foes along my way,
However bitter they may be,
So powerful to injure me
As I am, nor so quick to spoil
The beauty of my bit of toil.

Nobody harms me more than I;
   No one is meaner unto me;
Of all the foes that pass me by
   I am the worst one that I see.
I am the dangerous man to fear;
I am the cause of sorrow here;
Of all men 'gainst my hopes inclined
I am myself the most unkind.

I do more harmful things to me
   Than all the men who seem to hate;
I am the fellow that should be
   More dreaded than the works of fate.
I am the one that I must fight
With all my will and all my might;
My foes are better friends to me
Than I have ever proved to be.

I am the careless foe and mean;
　I am the selfish rival too;
My enmity to me is seen
　In almost everything I do.
More courage it requires to beat
Myself, than all the foes I meet;
I am more traitorous to me
Than other men could ever be.

In every struggle I have lost
　I am the one that was to blame;
My weaknesses cannot be glossed
　By glib excuses.　I was lame.
I that would dare for fame or pelf
Am far less daring with myself.
I care not who my foes may be,
I am my own worst enemy.

THE THINGS THAT HAVEN'T BEEN
DONE BEFORE

The things that haven't been done before,
  Those are the things to try;
Columbus dreamed of an unknown shore
  At the rim of the far-flung sky,
And his heart was bold and his faith was strong
  As he ventured in dangers new,
And he paid no heed to the jeering throng
  Or the fears of the doubting crew.

The many will follow the beaten track
  With guideposts on the way,
They live and have lived for ages back
  With a chart for every day.
Someone has told them it's safe to go
  On the road he has traveled o'er,
And all that they ever strive to know
  Are the things that were known before.

A few strike out, without map or chart,
  Where never a man has been,
From the beaten paths they draw apart
  To see what no man has seen.
There are deeds they hunger alone to do;
  Though battered and bruised and sore,
They blaze the path for the many, who
  Do nothing not done before.

The things that haven't been done before
　　Are the tasks worth while to-day;
Are you one of the flock that follows, or
　　Are you one that shall lead the way?
Are you one of the timid souls that quail
　　At the jeers of a doubting crew,
Or dare you, whether you win or fail,
　　Strike out for a goal that's new?

REVENGE

If I had hatred in my heart toward my fellow
　　man,
If I were pressed to do him ill, to conjure up a
　　plan
To wound him sorely and to rob his days of all
　　their joy,
I'd wish his wife would go away and take their
　　little boy.

I'd waste no time on curses vague, nor try to
　　take his gold,
Nor seek to shatter any plan that he might
　　dearly hold.
A crueler revenge than that for him I would
　　bespeak:
I'd wish his wife and little one might leave him
　　for a week.

I'd wish him all the loneliness that comes with
    loss of those
Who fill his life with laughter and contentment
    and repose.
I'd wish him empty rooms at night and mocking
    stairs to squeak
That neither wife nor little boy will greet him
    for a week.

If I despised my fellow man, I'd make my
    hatred known
By wishing him a week or two of living all
    alone;
I'd let him know the torture that is mine to
    bear to-day,
For Buddy and his mother now are miles and
    miles away.

PROMOTION

Promotion comes to him who sticks
Unto his work and never kicks,
Who watches neither clock nor sun
To tell him when his task is done;
Who toils not by a stated chart,
Defining to a jot his part,
But gladly does a little more
Than he's remunerated for.

The man, in factory or shop,
Who rises quickly to the top,
Is he who gives what can't be bought:
Intelligent and careful thought.

No one can say just when begins
The service that promotion wins,
Or when it ends; 'tis not defined
By certain hours or any kind
Of system that has been devised;
Merit cannot be systemized.
It is at work when it's at play;
It serves each minute of the day;
'Tis always at its post, to see
New ways of help and use to be.
Merit from duty never slinks,
Its cardinal virtue is — it thinks!

Promotion comes to him who tries
Not solely for a selfish prize,
But day by day and year by year
Holds his employer's interests dear.
Who measures not by what he earns
The sum of labor he returns,
Nor counts his day of toiling through
Till he's done all that he can do.
His strength is not of muscle bred,
But of the heart and of the head.
The man who would the top attain
Must demonstrate he has a brain.

EXPECTATION

Most folks, as I've noticed, in pleasure an'
    strife,
Are always expecting too much out of life.
    They wail an' they fret
    Just because they don't get
The best o' the sunshine, the fairest o' flowers,
The finest o' features, the strongest o' powers;
They whine an' they whimper an' curse an'
    condemn,
Coz life isn't always bein' partial to them.

Notwithstandin' the pain an' the sufferin' they
    see,
They cling to the notion that they should go
    free:
    That they shouldn't share
    In life's trouble an' care
But should always be happy an' never perplexed,
An' never discouraged or beaten or vexed.
When life treats 'em roughly an' jolts 'em with
    care,
They seem to imagine it's bein' unfair.

It's a curious notion folks hold in their pride,
That their souls should never be tested or tried;
    That others must mourn
    An' be sick an' forlorn

176

An' stand by the biers of their loved ones an'
    weep,
But life from such sorrows their bosoms must
    keep.
Oh, they mustn't know what it means to be sad,
Or they'll wail that the treatment they're gettin'
    is bad.

Now life as I view it means pleasure an' pain,
An' laughter an' weepin' an' sunshine an' rain,
        An' takin' an' givin';
        An' all who are livin'
Must face it an' bear it the best that they can
Believin' great Wisdom is workin' the plan.
An' no one should ever complain it's unfair
Because at the moment he's tastin' despair.

HARD WORK

One day, in ages dark and dim,
    A toiler, weary, worn and faint,
Who found his task too much for him,
    Gave voice unto a sad complaint.
And seeking emphasis to give
    Unto his trials (day ill-starred!)
Coupled to " work " this adjective,
    This little word of terror: *Hard.*

And from that day to this has work
   Its frightening description worn;
'Tis spoken daily by the shirk,
   The first cloud on the sky at morn.
To-day when there are tasks to do,
   Save that we keep ourselves on guard
With fearful doubtings them we view,
   And think and speak of them as hard.

That little but ill-chosen word
   Has wrought great havoc with men's souls,
Has chilled the hearts ambition stirred
   And held the pass to splendid goals.
Great dreams have faded and been lost,
   Fine youth by it been sadly marred
As plants beneath a withering frost,
   Because men thought and whispered: "Hard."

Let's think of work in terms of hope
   And speak of it with words of praise,
And tell the joy it is to grope
   Along the new, untrodden ways!
Let's break this habit of despair
   And cheerfully our task regard;
The road to happiness lies there:
   Why think or speak of it as hard?

GRATITUDE

Be grateful for the kindly friends that walk
  along your way;
Be grateful for the skies of blue that smile
  from day to day;
Be grateful for the health you own, the work
  you find to do,
For round about you there are men less fortu-
  nate than you.

Be grateful for the growing trees, the roses
  soon to bloom,
The tenderness of kindly hearts that shared your
  days of gloom;
Be grateful for the morning dew, the grass
  beneath your feet,
The soft caresses of your babes and all their
  laughter sweet.

Acquire the grateful habit, learn to see how blest
  you are,
How much there is to gladden life, how little
  life to mar!
And what if rain shall fall to-day and you with
  grief are sad;
Be grateful that you can recall the joys that
  you have had.

A REAL MAN

Men are of two kinds, and he
Was of the kind I'd like to be.
Some preach their virtues, and a few
Express their lives by what they do.
That sort was he. No flowery phrase
Or glibly spoken words of praise
Won friends for him. He wasn't cheap
Or shallow, but his course ran deep,
And it was pure. You know the kind.
Not many in a life you find
Whose deeds outrun their words so far
That more than what they seem they are.

There are two kinds of lies as well:
The kind you live, the ones you tell.
Back through his years from age to youth
He never acted one untruth.
Out in the open light he fought
And didn't care what others thought
Nor what they said about his fight
If he believed that he was right.
The only deeds he ever hid
Were acts of kindness that he did.

What speech he had was plain and blunt.
His was an unattractive front.
Yet children loved him; babe and boy
Played with the strength he could employ,

Without one fear, and they are fleet
To sense injustice and deceit.
No back door gossip linked his name
With any shady tale of shame.
He did not have to compromise
With evil-doers, shrewd and wise,
And let them ply their vicious trade
Because of some past escapade.

Men are of two kinds, and he
Was of the kind I'd like to be.
No door at which he ever knocked
Against his manly form was locked.
If ever man on earth was free
And independent, it was he.
No broken pledge lost him respect,
He met all men with head erect,
And when he passed I think there went
A soul to yonder firmament
So white, so splendid and so fine
It came almost to God's design.

THE NEIGHBORLY MAN

Some are eager to be famous, some are striving
    to be great,
Some are toiling to be leaders of their nation
    or their state,
And in every man's ambition, if we only under-
    stood,
There is much that's fine and splendid; every
    hope is mostly good.
So I cling unto the notion that contented I
    will be
If the men upon life's pathway find a needed
    friend in me.

I rather like to putter 'round the walks and
    yards of life,
To spray at night the roses that are burned and
    browned with strife;
To eat a frugal dinner, but always to have a
    chair
For the unexpected stranger that my simple
    meal would share.
I don't care to be a traveler, I would rather be
    the one
Sitting calmly by the roadside helping weary
    travelers on.

I'd like to be a neighbor in the good old-fashioned way,
Finding much to do for others, but not over
   much to say.
I like to read the papers, but I do not yearn
   to see
What the journal of the morning has been
   moved to say of me;
In the silences and shadows I would live my
   life and die
And depend for fond remembrance on some
   grateful passers-by.

I guess I wasn't fashioned for the brilliant
   things of earth,
Wasn't gifted much with talent or designed for
   special worth,
But was just sent here to putter with life's little
   odds and ends
And keep a simple corner where the stirring
   highway bends,
And if folks should chance to linger, worn and
   weary through the day,
To do some needed service and to cheer them
   on their way.

ROSES

When God first viewed the rose He'd made
    He smiled, and thought it passing fair;
Upon the bloom His hands He laid,
    And gently blessed each petal there.
He summoned in His artists then
    And bade them paint, as ne'er before,
Each petal, so that earthly men
    Might love the rose for evermore.

With Heavenly brushes they began
    And one with red limned every leaf,
To signify the love of man;
    The first rose, white, betokened grief;
"My rose shall deck the bride," one said
    And so in pink he dipped his brush,
"And it shall smile beside the dead
    To typify the faded blush."

And then they came unto His throne
    And laid the roses at His feet,
The crimson bud, the bloom full blown,
    Filling the air with fragrance sweet.
"Well done, well done!" the Master spake;
    "Henceforth the rose shall bloom on earth:
One fairer blossom I will make,"
    And then a little babe had birth.

On earth a loving mother lay
    Within a rose-decked room and smiled,
But from the blossoms turned away
    To gently kiss her little child,
And then she murmured soft and low,
    " For beauty, here, a mother seeks.
None but the Master made, I know,
    The roses in a baby's cheeks."

THE JUNK BOX

My father often used to say:
" My boy don't throw a thing away:
You'll find a use for it some day."

So in a box he stored up things,
Bent nails, old washers, pipes and rings,
And bolts and nuts and rusty springs.

Despite each blemish and each flaw,
Some use for everything he saw;
With things material, this was law.

And often when he'd work to do,
He searched the junk box through and through
And found old stuff as good as new.

And I have often thought since then,
That father did the same with men;
He knew he'd need their help again.

It seems to me he understood
That men, as well as iron and wood,
May broken be and still be good.

Despite the vices he'd display
He never threw a man away,
But kept him for another day.

A human junk box is this earth
And into it we're tossed at birth,
To wait the day we'll be of worth.

Though bent and twisted, weak of will,
And full of flaws and lacking skill,
Some service each can render still.

THE BOY THAT WAS

When the hair about the temples starts to show
    the signs of gray,
And a fellow realizes that he's wandering far
    away
From the pleasures of his boyhood and his
    youth, and never more
Will know the joy of laughter as he did in days
    of yore,

Oh, it's then he starts to thinking of a stubby
    little lad
With a face as brown as berries and a soul
    supremely glad.

When a gray-haired dreamer wanders down the
    lanes of memory
And forgets the living present for the time of
    " used-to-be,"
He takes off his shoes and stockings, and he
    throws his coat away,
And he's free from all restrictions, save the rules
    of manly play.
He may be in richest garments, but bareheaded
    in the sun
He forgets his proud successes and the riches
    he has won.

Oh, there's not a man alive but that would give
    his all to be
The stubby little fellow that in dreamland he
    can see,
And the splendors that surround him and the
    joys about him spread
Only seem to rise to taunt him with the boyhood
    that has fled.
When the hair about the temples starts to show
    Time's silver stain,
Then the richest man that's living yearns to be
    a boy again.

AS FALL THE LEAVES

As fall the leaves, so drop the days
  In silence from the tree of life;
Born for a little while to blaze
  In action in the heat of strife,
And then to shrivel with Time's blast
And fade forever in the past.

In beauty once the leaf was seen;
  To all it offered gentle shade;
Men knew the splendor of its green
  That cheered them so, would quickly fade:
And quickly, too, must pass away
All that is splendid of to-day.

To try to keep the leaves were vain:
  Men understand that they must fall;
Why should they bitterly complain
  When sorrows come to one and all?
Why should they mourn the passing day
That must depart along the way?

INDEX OF FIRST LINES